Praise for
Eloise J. Knapp

"Eloise shows the reader a funhouse mirror, where humanity's reflection shines back dark and perverse."
—Charnel House Reviews.com

"...Eloise J. Knapp once again shows why she is one of the zombie genre's rising stars. Original, sharp and filled with enough violence and grossouts to satisfy even the most jaded zombie fan, PULSE is a fast burn that delivers."
—Craig DiLouie, author of SUFFER THE CHILDREN

"It's downright cold-hearted and shockingly brutal—and virtually unputdownable."
—Paul "Goat" Allen, Barnes and Noble

"Brilliantly unusual characters are the reason that [The Undead Situation] stands out. Bluntly put...I've never so thoroughly enjoyed a book full of people that I can't stand."
—Jill McDole, Impact Online

PULSE

Eloise J. Knapp

Pulse copyright © 2014
By Eloise J. Knapp
All Rights Reserved.

Cover art by Eloise J. Knapp.

This book is a work of fiction. People, places, events, and situations are the product of the author's imagination. Any resemblance to actual persons, living, or dead, or historical events, is purely coincidental.

Without limiting the rights under copyright reserved above, no part of this publication may be reproduced, stored, or introduced into a retrieval system, or transmitted in any form, or by any means, without prior written permission of the copyright owner, expect in the case of brief quotations within critical articles and reviews.

For all the people who listen when I say,
"Did I tell you about my latest idea?"

Prologue

Garrett Miller had been fishing the Pacific since his daddy took him and his brother on the water and said, 'Get to work.' They'd learned even the worst catch was still a catch, and throwing it back didn't do no one any good. He had never considered throwing something back unless he really had to, or being completely honest at the market. Not once.

Plus, as long as you told the kids in Seattle that it was locally sourced (it was), and sustainable (he wasn't sure what that meant) they'd pay top dollar thinking they were doing a good deed. They *were* doing something good. Garrett had five children and a wife at home to take care of. He never finished high school since fishing was what his family had always done. He felt that there weren't any options for him, which is how he justified the occasional underhanded deal. If the market wouldn't take them, they sold it to a dealer who shipped fish across the country.

But on a gray, lifeless day, when the net came up and the fish were barely flopping, he got a sick feeling in his stomach that something wasn't right. Some of them were downright dead. Others had eyeballs that were burst or bloody red. A handful of them reeked and their bellies were blown out, the guts and most of the meat gone.

Ever since the nuclear disaster in Fukushima, Garrett's wife Pat welcomed him home with the latest news story she'd read online. Garrett indulged her the first few times, listening to her proclamation that fishing was dangerous, and that radiation was being carried in fish and the currents all the way to Washington. Once she went so far as to boycott anything from the sea in the house. He wouldn't admit it, but much of what she said *did* scare him, so when the strange fish came up in the net, Garrett felt a dreadful sense of confirmation rather than surprise.

He didn't say a word to his brother Mark, who eyed the catch, his gloved hands on his hips. "Toss the dead ones."

Relief flooded Garrett at his brother's command. He began hauling the net up when Mark stopped him.

"No, just toss the dead ones. We'll salvage the others, cut the heads off and sell 'em to Ron. Trust me little bro, these fish will be half way across the country and not our problem in a few days."

"They're gross looking," Garrett said. "No one would eat these."

Mark prodded a fish with his boot, then stared Garrett down. "Pat's been on your case about Christmas, right? We're all strapped for cash. No sense in letting 'em go to waste."

Garrett didn't like it. Times were tough, but they'd never seen fish in such bad shape before. He hesitated. If something happened, it might come back to him. Things would be a hell of a lot worse then. What would Pat think if she knew he was sending radiated monster fish into the world?

He steeled himself against the thought. It was all conspiracy. He knew better than to let Pat's crazy get to him. Plus, staring into his older brother's unforgiving eyes, he knew he'd couldn't say no. He didn't call the shots.

He threw the dead ones back in the water, putting the rest on ice.

1 The Infected

In a podunk little town in North Dakota a man named Jay Lehmann died. He had no children to his name and never married. His best friend was a bottle of the cheapest whiskey he could find. Calling him the town drunk would be giving him too much credit; really, no one knew him well enough to bestow a title.

Four days prior to Jay's death, he bought a slice of salmon on quick sale from the town store. The store didn't usually get fish, being so far away from water and all. Even at its best by the time the salmon arrived, it was old.

It was a real treat, but he felt like he deserved it after the bad summer. Jay pawned a ring he found while plowing his field and made thirty bucks which meant he was celebrating. The color of the fish looked a little off, but he had a stomach of iron like his momma always said. Only gotten food poisoning twice in his life, so there was no sense in wasting a good piece of fish. He seared both sides and ate it chewy in the middle, how he liked his fish.

After that he got sick. Sicker than he'd ever been before. Yellow, thick sweat oozed from his pores and was sticky to the touch. Blood vessels popped in his eyes until there were no whites. On the third day he fell into a coma. On the fourth day he woke up.

And wanted to kill.

An agonizing pain coursed through his body, sending spasms through his arms and legs. Thoughts of every person in town who looked at him wrong flooded his mind. All he could think of was tearing their bodies apart with his teeth, hearing their screams as he took their lives away.

Jay Lehmann got to his feet, ran out the door of his one room shack, and began looking for someone to rip apart and eat alive. He went back to the very grocery store he bought the fish from and tore into shoppers with the ferocity of an animal.

***

Later, in a tiny emergency clinic in North Dakota, twenty miles from the grocery store incident with Jay Lehmann, ten patients came in with symptoms none of the small town doctors had ever seen before. The complete reddening of the eyes and foul sticky sweat, culminating in a coma...it was too much for them to handle.

They were unaware they needed to inform the CDC of multiple similar cases with symptoms like these. They were unaware of what their breach in protocol meant for the nation. Instead, they stuck IVs in them, began running as many tests as they knew of, and prayed for the best. The sheriff insisted the town didn't need any more bad attention, so they locked down the hospital and let no one from the media in.

Little did they know, had they contacted the CDC, the beginning of the end would never have happened.

2 Dom

"Do you know what would be amazing?"

"Huh?"

"The zombie apocalypse," Dom said. He lowered his voice, glancing around the break room to verify he was alone. He switched the phone to his other ear. "I don't know if I can stand another day working here. It isn't even the customers. It's my manager. She's killing me."

Chelsea laughed. "Well yeah, of course. Everyone wants the zombie apocalypse to happen. And man up, we all have bad managers. That's life."

"Some girlfriend you are. I thought you were supposed to comfort me? Tell me I'm better than this and give me some hope." Dom was teasing. He and Chelsea shared a lovingly sarcastic sense of humor that many of their friends didn't get.

"Don't be an ass, Dom." She paused after laughing. "I think it could happen. Zombies. It would be viral though. Nothing unexplained or paranormal or whatever."

Dom took a swig of his energy drink and checked the clock. Breaks were never long enough. "True. But realistically the government would take them out pretty quick, virus or magic."

"No way. It would get out of control too fast. We'd be screwed. Well, not me. I have a shotgun and like three weeks of food at least," she said.

"I've seen your house. You have a week tops. I could go two months maybe. Got the assault rifle, a shotgun, and food."

"Dominick, your break is over." Anne, his manager, stood in the break room doorframe tapping her foot. The day he found another job would be a happy day. That's where the zombie apocalypse fantasy always came into play.

"Gotta go, break's over. Those lattes won't make themselves."

"Come see me tonight?"

"We'll see. Love you."

***

Dom finished his shift, clocked out, and headed home. It was raining, making the weekend traffic in Seattle more of a nightmare than usual. Something about the rain made everyone driving a vehicle lose it. In the span of twenty minute he saw a truck hit a parked car in a botched parallel park and two fender benders. It was so absurd he found himself laughing.

A group of girls in short dresses waiting under an awning of a club pointedly looked away from him, like people did to the homeless. Embarrassed, he quickened his pace.

He was damp and in a mood by the time he got back to his apartment. Some days he could zone out and get through a day of work quickly without much thought. Others, like today, it took the life out of him. He was in need of total solitude for the rest of the day to recoup.

When he entered the apartment complex lobby he saw his neighbor's sleazy boyfriend waiting for the elevator. The guy was a total jerk and tried to pick fights with anyone who looked at him. Dom veered off to the stairwell and hoofed it up four flights of steps. Better that than spend a minute in a closed space with him.

Breathless from the stairs, Dom opened the door to find his roommate reclined on the couch, eyes glued to the TV. The house smelled rotten and vaguely of spoiled milk under the scent of pizza, which meant—despite his repeated texts to remind him—Brian hadn't taken out the garbage. Two boxes of pizza were open on the counter. Brian liked hacking the online ordering system when a two topping special was in effect; he put two different toppings on each half of a pizza, totaling four different flavors. Dom spotted his favorite combination—pineapple and pepperoni—and felt a little less angry towards Brian.

Brian worked part time at Gamestop in the mall, but mostly lived off money from his parents. He was allegedly taking classes online, but Dom had yet to see him spend any time on the internet not devoted to watching videos.

Sure, rent was always paid on time, but Dom didn't like coming home to a messy house and Brian doing nothing, even if he *did* order pizza. Every time he felt that twinge of irritation come over him, he reminded himself that's how his dad was and it got nobody anywhere. Plus, technically he wasn't leaps and bounds better than Brian on the education front so he couldn't judge him too much. Dom finished community college with intent to transfer to the University of Washington, but his grades weren't good enough for a scholarship and financial aid wouldn't cover all his expenses.

Dom was the first person to admit his life needed a catalyst; something that could reboot him and motivate him to get going.

Brian barely glanced at Dom. "You won't believe this."

Dom shrugged off his jacket and hung it on the back of the door. "Yeah? What?"

"Just…just watch."

7

He kicked off his shoes and came over, grabbing a slice of pizza from the counter as he went. It was still warm and he savored every bite, the fat and carbs already making him feel better.

"...unknown white male in his sixties came into a grocery store and attacked ten people. The man was reportedly shot four times before he finally went down. Three are dead, the rest wounded. And now, Walter with the weather."

"So? A tragic violent incident. The news eats those up, exaggerates them, and spits them back out," Dom said. There were cups of ranch dressing on the coffee table. Dom snatched one up and dipped his pizza into it.

Brian's jaw dropped. "Are you serious, man?"

"Yeah."

"They had to shoot him four times before he went down. And plus, watch this." He clicked the back button and rewound the news. "The people he attacked had bites on them."

He paused on a scene of two women limping from a small grocery store. The footage was shaky, probably from a cell. One clutched her neck. Red cascaded down her front. The other woman had what appeared to be bite marks on her arm. Well, *could have been* bite marks. Dom was already projecting what Brian said.

"You don't know they're bites. It didn't specify how the man attacked them. If he had a knife, it would cause a lot of blood. He could've scratched them, too. Besides, are you trying to say this was—"

"Zombies. Damn straight I am. I mean the evidence is obvious!"

Dom wasn't sure how to react. Obviously he wanted to think it was zombies. The fluttering in his chest was excitement, panic, and denial all at once. He remembered bath salts a while back, and how a guy ate another guy's face off or something. Everyone thought it was zombies. That was more 'zombie' than this. Yet no one truly did anything. No riots, no panic. This would be the same thing.

Plus, there was such a huge fixation on zombies lately it was in everyone's mind. Hell, he was just talking to Chelsea about it.

But something about the shaky footage of the women running from the building made him feel uneasy. It was in a remote farming area; the news barely said anything about it. They hadn't explained how an old man could attack that many people before someone stopped him. It seemed the report was carefully *unexaggerated.*

His phone chimed. It was a text from Chelsea.

Did you see the news?

Yeah. Dom typed. **Probably nothing**

Still scary. Sleeping with the shotgun by me tonight

"So, stock up on ammo and board up the place?" Brian changed the channel to the Food Network, apparently having lost interest. Dramatize something, act like it's the end of the world, then watch someone do a seafood boil? That was Brian.

Dom walked off to his room, grabbing another slice of pizza on the way. "Yeah, good luck with that."

3 Adam

Adam Baker wasn't a religious man. He believed in the power of what was real and what was now. With that mindset, he was always at the top of all his classes—not just scientifically oriented ones—from the time he was in grade school through getting his PhD in biochemistry at the University of Washington. It also helped him avoid thinking about higher powers, fate, and other intangible topics as he excelled in subjects that truly meant something to the world.

That could make a difference, he always thought, remembering what his high school chemistry teacher always said. These days that kind of talk might come off as antireligious and get you kicked out of the job. Adam hated that. It was why he had no interest in becoming a professor, no matter how deep his love for learning; he wouldn't sacrifice truth or integrity for anything. More than a handful of professors he had in college carefully skirted around issues on occasion, avoiding offending students. Only the tenured professors seemed to say what they wanted. Adam didn't want to tiptoe around students until he earned tenure. It seemed like a huge waste of intellect.

With his knowledge, determination, and love for biology, he was confident his passion would lead him to new discoveries and work in the field of biological warfare. He had big dreams and a lot of plans. But he didn't plan for Gina.

Gina wouldn't have been his first choice for a girlfriend. She was getting her undergrad in psychology with a double major in philosophy (an absolute joke to him, and a source of contention in their relationship even to date) and seemed like kind of a flake. Adam met her at the second 'real' college party he'd ever been to—and *real* meant not Dungeons and Dragons night or Theoretical Science Night with his colleagues.

The only reason he was there was because he was a popular biology tutor among the frat brothers, and they felt obligated to invite him so he could 'get laid' and 'join the real world.' The primary sounded good, the latter a joke considering most of the frat guys would go nowhere in life.

Looking back, the fact that a semi-attractive girl was speaking to him clouded his perception of Gina. He tried to tell himself her double major was impressive, but she held a low GPA and couldn't carry on a conversation about anything beyond who she saw at Starbucks, who such-and-such was with, and who slept with who for a better grade. The problem was that Adam had never had a girlfriend.

At all. Ever.

His looks got him in the door, but his awkward and shy personality sent him right back out. In high school and all of his college years, girls liked to flirt with him yet keep him perpetually in the friend zone. His lack of experience made him a perfect target for a girl like Gina; he was easy to manipulate, especially once sex was involved.

After a year of dating she got pregnant, with twins to make it even worse. Adam's deepest fear was being a father, not because he disliked children, but because it meant he'd have to sacrifice his own personal agenda to raise them. Growing up, his mother sacrificed her sense of autonomy for him and his father worked endless hours as a mechanic to support them.

Yet Gina convinced him to marry her and, well, it's the same old story from there.

Upon graduating, he tried to follow his heart in experimental research despite having a wife and children to take care of. It was invigorating, meaningful work and the best time of his life. But Gina wore away at him for years, complaining constantly about money and security, until he caved and began applying to higher paying, "stable" jobs. The offer to work for the CDC was exactly what she'd been waiting for.

Even though it meant uprooting their lives in Seattle and moving almost three thousand miles away to Georgia, she insisted it was the only logical thing to do. Adam hated the idea of it. He loved Seattle; its landscape, culture, and people. Leaving it—or dating Gina, if you look that far back—was the worst decision he'd ever made. But he wouldn't leave his daughters without a father, and Gina would slaughter him in the courts anyway. She was good like that, putting on a show and saying whatever she had to in order to get her way.

Plus the twins had already joined their mother's side. Adam tried getting them interested in any type of science possible, but Gina simply had more time to cater them into carbon copies of herself. They thought Adam was an idiot by the age of three.

As he reviewed what information he had on the outbreak of a virus in North Dakota, he never felt as remorseful about his mistakes in life. If he hadn't gone to that party, he wouldn't be in Georgia dealing with the worst incident of his career.

Even though he understood the North Dakota incident was probably some kind of biological warfare tactic, or bizarre form of human rabies, his mind had a way of making it personal. Insult to injury. Rubbing salt in the wound. This had only happened since he was there.

But feelings were something he didn't like dwelling on, especially when they seemed to be rooted in irrational thoughts. He took to shuffling papers on his desk and rearranging his drawers—making a determined effort to wipe thoughts of his past transgressions away—considering what he knew about the case before he got down to writing reports and authorizing tests.

He took out his yellow legal pad and set down a pen, scrawling 'Facts' on the top. A trick his mother taught him was, when feeling overwhelmed, to simply write down what he knew to be true so he could ground himself. Adam took that advice to heart and always did it on difficult cases.

The old man, Jay Lehmann, attacked a grocery store full of people and was reported to have been shouting unintelligible words and exhibited erratic movements. The people he'd attacked began showing similar symptoms after a short period of time.

Some bodies retrieved from the scene were chewed up, the bites from human teeth. Others were mutilated by surgical tools, raped, or showed signs of other torture. The range of deaths were broad, so much so that it obviously pointed to some kind of loss of brain function rooted in the individual. It seemed there was no other way to explain why there was such variety in the murders. Perhaps a chemical imbalance caused by the virus?

Those were the facts. He let his mind wander into dangerous territory: speculation.

Why release it in such a small area? If it was biological warfare it would've made the most sense to release it in a densely populated area. Based on patient zero's age and location, Adam would've argued him the *worst* candidate for such a thing. Yes, Lehmann did make it to the grocery store. He did infect other people. But so much could've gone wrong. It might never have worked. If it was an act of war, it would've started in a big city.

Whenever the sinking anxiety and fear of the unknown got to him, he let anger take over. If the doctors at that hospital had followed protocol and informed the CDC about the unusual behavior early on with Lehmann's victims, they might have been able to stop the spread in its tracks. Five similar cases warranted a call to the CDC, yet not a single email was sent or a phone called.

Now there was an epidemic on their hands. The virus was spreading through North Dakota like wildfire. According to the files they retrieved remotely from the hospital's network, patients initially fell into a coma for two days. On the third, they became extremely violent towards others and themselves. After that, they could only rely on security video to see anything else.

But the virus was spreading much faster than what the three day timeline reported from the hospital should have been capable of. It only took a matter of a day or two after transmission for the virus to reach *full form* and patients to begin losing control. Police and hospital reports from adjacent towns were flooding the CDC; none of them said anything new or helpful. It was the same case report over and over: someone was acting insane, harming themselves and others. They were forcibly detained.

Detaining these crazy people would only work for so long. From the police reports Adam read, they'd often kill each other in jail cells. They'd run out of room eventually, plus the threat of the officers being around infected persons was undeniably risky.

Adam wrote the word *dangerous* on his notepad, underlining it three times. "This isn't a drill," he said aloud, mimicking a line from one of his favorite movies.

Whatever it was, it was strong. Smart. The hosts were immune to sedation and were resistant to physical harm. The only thing to stop them thus far had been multiple gunshot wounds, incineration, or full destruction of the brain. Their behavior was similar to those infected with Mad Cow or rabies, but tenfold. The consumption of human flesh was unsettling, but it appeared to be an act of violence rather than a desire to consume. And the sadistic violence he'd seen in the videos...

The memory hit him before he could block it out. Two women dragging a doctor into a hallway in the ER. Their bodies twitched, heads snapping left and right as though they had no control. One beat his head into the ground while the other removed his leg with a bone saw.

Adam took a breath, his fingers hovering over the keyboard at his computer as he prepared to write a report. The facts weren't proving to be as reassuring as they had been in the past. Whatever was happening, it was unlike anything he'd ever seen. In this case, there was cause for alarm, speculation, fact gathering; anything a person could dream up.

He began typing, advising they make an official announcement as soon as possible, and reviewing each bit of concrete information they knew so far.

He glanced at the word 'dangerous' on his notepad.

Adam wasn't a religious man, but he was considering a life change.

4 Price Family

Lindsey Price's daughter Sally fell off her swing set and complained she had pain in her arm. The five year old had developed a tendency to dramatize lately, and she claimed it was broken. If it weren't for the fact that she said the very same thing about her leg last week, they would've taken her to the hospital the instant it happened.

But since Sam lost his job they didn't have health insurance and the trip to the hospital would cost them dearly for another alleged broken limb. His on and off farm and landscaping work was barely enough to get them by as it was.

It took an hour of discussion before Lindsey resolved to ask her parents for money if they weren't able to get a good payment plan for whatever bills they incurred.

"We are not bad parents," Lindsey told Sam firmly. "I can't believe we waited this long."

Sam had a job that day, so Lindsey went alone. When they arrived, something was off. It was the attitude the staff had; distant and irritated. The nurse was on edge as she took Sally's weight and height, her mind elsewhere. Lindsey asked her a question regarding Sally's height just to see if she was paying attention, if Sally was meeting the average height for her age, and the nurse didn't even answer. When the doctor came in he had the same attitude.

"Do I get a lollipop after?" Lindsey asked him, her tone commanding. "I got one last time I was here, and mom and dad don't let me have sugar at home. She had to ask twice before the doctor shook himself as though coming out of a daze and nodded.

"Of course. I've got red, blue, and orange."

She pursed her lips, displeased with the options. "I like green."

Lindsey rubbed Sally's back, wanting to speed up the exam. If they weren't going to give her the time of day, she didn't want to be here. The sooner they could get an X-ray and find out if her arm was broken, the sooner they could leave. In the meantime, she had to derail the oncoming tantrum Sally was about to have.

"Honey, you like blue, too."

Her daughter shrugged. "Green."

The doctor glanced at the door. Lindsey set her jaw, glaring at the doctor as she told Sally, "We'll get you ten green lollipops at the store on the way home."

"Ok." She smiled.

The doctor wasn't amused. He'd only just began checking out her arm when the commotion started. At first it was a series of scuffles, then it sounded like people were knocking things over.

The doctor excused himself from the exam room in a rush. Lindsey cracked the door open to catch a glimpse of whatever was going on. When she saw the crazy people and the blood, she knew she had to get her and her daughter to safety.

She told Sally to be brave. She carried her down the hall, eyes darting about. Nurses were panicking, racing to and from rooms. The screaming was picking up. Sally was crying about pain in her arm. But all she focused on was getting out.

As she rounded a corner she slipped and came crashing down. Sally fell from her arms face first into a pool of blood.

"Mom! Mom, I can't see!"

Lindsey picked her up and wiped as much blood from her daughter's face as she could. "I know baby, we're

17

leaving. It's going to be okay. I have boogie wipes in the car."

"Mom, it tastes gross," Sally cried. Spit and blood dribbled from her mouth. "I want to go home! I want to go home *now!*"

In front of them a crazed woman stood behind the reception desk. Her chest heaved as she breathed. Blood and spit spattered from her mouth. Lindsey bolted passed her and out the doors, praying she wouldn't pursue.

They made it out and to the car just as police were swarming the building. Lindsey asked for help, but three people ran from the hospital and began attacking the police. When the deafening roar of gunfire began, she knew there was no help for her there.

Neither of them were hurt, besides Sally's arm. She took Sally home and cleaned her up, researching home remedies for temporarily aiding broken limbs until they could get to a doctor. Each time Lindsey thought of the event, trying to make sense of it, it was a blur. She put her attention to making sure Sally was comfortable, bringing her water with ice chips in her favorite princess cup and making sure her stuffed animals were arranged to her liking.

When she finally fell asleep, Lindsey retreated to the office where she began calling every doctor's office in town that she could, researching the nearest hospitals. Sam never kept his phone on him during work, making her feel alone.

What a mess, she thought as another recorded message told her the office was closed. She set down the phone. The other private doctor's offices around town weren't answering. All they could do was make the trip to the nearest ER, nearly sixty miles away. At times like this Lindsey cursed living in such a remote area.

Sam spent his entire life in only a few towns in North Dakota doing farm work. He came to Boston to help his high school friend remodel a house, which is where he met Lindsey. She fell in love with him the day she met him. His time in Boston went from a couple months to a year and they got married. Sam wanted to return to North Dakota, convincing her it was a great place to raise the child she was pregnant with. She agreed.

After the miscarriage he started drinking. Lindsey didn't blame him. Words couldn't describe the depression she spiraled into afterwards. It took years before they tried again. When Sally was born, Sam got sober and they resumed their lives.

She went into her daughter's room. The afternoon light cut though the blinds and illuminated her sickly form. The bedding was soaked. The acrid stench of sweat and what smelled like rot almost choked her. Lindsey's pulse quickened. Her palms grew damp.

Sally had a fever and was sweating heavily. She'd shown no signs of being sick when they got home, but it seemed like she was in the throes of an awful flu.

"Sweetie? We're going to take you to a different doctor, okay? Let's get you ready."

She sat on the bed and her daughter groaned.

"Mom, I don't feel good." She whimpered. "My belly hurts. Can you rub it?"

"Sure, of course." She peeled the blanket away and moved her hand in circular motions over her daughter's stomach. No matter how hard she tried, she couldn't suppress the nasty feeling of the slimy sweat against her skin.

Then she felt something moving. Undulating. As Lindsey lifted the shirt and beheld the skin shifting, as though something were alive beneath it, she saw spots then blackness as she fainted.

5 Dom

Two days after the North Dakota accident it became a blip on the news. Dom heard no customers at work speak of it. Normally the original Starbucks location in Pike Place was packed and a hub of conversation. Not a trace of it was on the news. Unlike what he suspected about it being sensationalized, the news seemed to run out of information to tell and repeated the same report, sometimes the wording or angle barely changed.

People on the internet still brought it up on occasion. There were a few memes, but none funny enough to pick up speed. Much of the panic buying of ammunition and food at local stores died down.

Things were almost back to normal when, on the third day since the incident, the seven remaining living victims went insane and began massacring people at a hospital. The news didn't need to sensationalize it. The footage they played nonstop on every station said it all.

Insanity wasn't an overstatement. It was exactly right.

Cell phones and leaked security footage captured scenes of brutal violence and gore. Bloodied, spastic aggressors tackled people to the floor and beat them. Sometimes they used their mouths and tore out huge chunks of flesh. They kept going until there was nothing but pulpy mess and broken bones left.

It would've been easy for Dom to plop down on the couch and surf every news channel for more details. For another personal story or new angle. To feed his morbid curiosity. He'd done it before with various murder cases or tragedies, but this time Dom stopped watching after the first ten minutes. He'd seen the worst horror movies. He'd played the most M-rated videogames. He considered himself desensitized to violence because of them. Yet what the TV was showing made him sick. This was worse than anything he could ever have imagined.

Desensitized? It was impossible to make yourself immune to the scene of a man beating a toddler's head against a counter.

The world started watching about an hour after it started happening. Eight hours later and most of them were probably still there, glued to it, basking in the chaos and tragedy. They were calling their loved ones, making sympathetic noises and talking about how terrible it all was.

Brian cycled through three news channels, his laptop, and his phone to maximize his information absorption rate.

Brian and Chelsea insisted it was a zombie apocalypse. For real. Viral. The man who attacked the people at the grocery store must have been infected and the ones he didn't kill were infected. Brian bet the reason why police weren't able to get it under control was because more people were being infected, their numbers growing. And it seemed true. The situation was spiraling out of control. If only seven people started the attack, and it was still going in an *entire* hospital, there had to be something escalating it.

Dom's stomach was tight and he felt on edge. He felt immense sorrow for the victims in the hospital, but at the same time...

Anne closed the coffee shop down early in respect for the incident and everyone got to go home early. If he didn't know what a heartless bitch she was, the gesture would've been good. But he knew she did it because it made her look like a good, sympathetic manager.

21

The potential zombie apocalypse had only just started and he was already benefiting from it. A free day off from work?

Dom mentally slapped himself. He was no better than the news channels profiting off the tragedy. There he was, drooling over a day off when people were killed over nothing.

He found himself wandering to the pantry and extra bedroom to check how much food and ammunition they had. He was right when he told Chelsea they had enough food for two months. If they rationed well. Growing up, his mother emphasized disaster preparedness and it stuck with him. He tilted a flat of soup from Costco to check the expiration date. It expired mid last year, but it was still good.

"I think we should get supplies."

Dom jumped at the sound of Brian's voice. He hadn't seen him move for any reason but to eat or relieve himself all day. "What?"

"The CDC just made a statement. Come look."

He followed his roommate to the living room, where something from CNN was paused.

Brian hit play and Dom watched the two minute announcement.

"Get your keys," Dom said, the second it was over. "We're going to Wal-Mart."

***

"Full quarantine on the entire state. Can you believe that?"

Dom shook his head. He was still trying to believe it. "There's no way they can stop it from leaving the state. If it's as bad as they said, once it reaches more populated areas it will snowball."

"That's why we're gearing up now," Brian said. The car swerved into the other lane. He wasn't a good driver to begin with; his emphatic hand motions as he spoke made it even worse.

The drive across I90 started to seem like a more dangerous venture than the task at hand. The nearest Wal-Mart was almost thirty minutes away, but it was the cheapest and most well stocked store. They could get everything they needed in one stop.

"I wish we started preparing sooner, to tell you the truth. Days ago." Dom sighed. "We've seen every zombie movie, read like every zombie book. If we were really serious we would've gotten food and ammo four days ago when this thing first started."

"Let it be known, I *did* say we should on the first day," Brian snapped.

He gritted his teeth. Brian had, but if he hadn't been so damn catty about it maybe Dom would've listened. Besides, he also held himself accountable. He thought about it, too.

"Anyway, remember bath salts?"

"Exactly. We didn't do anything to prepare," Dom said. He was glad Brian mentioned it; the blame went to both of them, then.

They coasted off their exit. Away from Seattle the roads were more spacious, the buildings shorter and farther apart.

"We didn't, but here is the huge difference: the government actually said we're in trouble. They're for real shutting down entire states!"

"Well, whatever the case I hope no one else is taking this as seriously as us," Dom said. "Because then we can get into Wal-Mart, load up on everything we can, and head home."

His phone chimed. **Did you see the news? I'm afraid.**

23

"And pick up Chelsea," Dom added, and began texting her back.

"Hey, Dom? I don't think the first part of that plan will be so easy."

He felt the car slow down and he looked up. There was a vehicle on fire in the Wal-Mart parking lot and a horde of frightened, desperate people fighting each other to get inside.

"Holy fu—"

Then the car door opened and he was being dragged out by a man with a gun.

"Give me what you have!"

The man with the gun said it over and over, pressing the muzzle into Dom's temple. The sounds of people shouting and metal shopping carts clinking were louder now. Dom was on his knees staring at Brian, pleading with his eyes for his roommate to do something.

But he didn't do anything. His face was blank, his body tense.

"We don't have anything," Dom said. The man kneed him in the back. Dom fell forward, his face slamming against the car door. He tasted blood as he bit his tongue. "We just got here, I swear!"

After an unintelligible grunt and another shove against Dom's back, he sprinted away into the crowd. Dom hauled himself into the car and locked the doors. Blood rushed to his head. He felt dizzy. He wanted to yell at Brian for not doing anything, for not even making a move to save him, for sitting there and staring like an idiot.

But now wasn't the time.

"We need to get out of here," he said. "Brian, are you listening? We need to go home."

The car on fire in the parking lot exploded. Bodies flew backward. Small bits of debris bounced off Brian's car. A stillness followed it, onlookers gawking, but only for a moment before the chaos resumed.

Brian regained his composure. He reversed the car and turned them around. As they drove, the city returned to normal. The incident appeared to be isolated to that one area.

"That was fucking insane." Dom's voice was hoarse. It was all he could think to say, but he needed to say something. Anything to fill the empty silence.

"Yeah," Brian finally said. "Yeah, it really was. Like a movie or something."

There he was. That was Brian, Dom thought, finding a way to make it not so scary. On any other day he would hate it, but in that moment it was what he needed. Dom laughed, uneasy but ready to lighten the mood.

"A Danny Boyle movie, right?"

Brian chuckled. "Yeah. Really though, we need to try and get some supplies before *that* is happening everywhere. Stock up, remember?"

"There's a Fred Meyer a few miles away from the movie theater. Let's try there before we start the drive back to Seattle."

As they drove, Dom compiled a list on his phone. It was somber at first; water, canned foods, dried foods, medical supplies. Then they started joking. Cherry and blackberry fruit pies, all the red vines the store has, condoms just in case. It went on until they were laughing hysterically. Brian almost ran a stop sign and the festivity ended.

Even once they parked and exited the car it felt normal. It was in stark contrast to the Wal-Mart. There wasn't a hint of anything amiss until they were inside the store. No regular sized shopping carts; Dom and Brian each took a half-sized, glad they didn't have to resort to hand baskets. There were few cashiers, a fraction of the lanes open, but people were still being orderly.

Impatient, but orderly.

It was easy to start blocking out what they'd seen at Wal-Mart. It was a fluke. Maybe it didn't have anything to do with the infection? Dom thought of the stereotype of people that went to Wal-Mart. Blame it on that? God, what about Black Friday? It wasn't totally out of the realm of possibility people would act like that.

They decided to hit the canned food aisles first. Most of the quick foods were gone, like chili and soup. Canned vegetables and broths were much more plentiful.

"Who's gonna cook this stuff? I guess we'll need to print some recipes off the internet before we don't *have* the internet," Dom joked.

"You can be the wife." Brian reorganized his basket to fit more corn and beets. "You handle all that domestic stuff and I'll take care of...ah, repairs and defense and whatnot."

"Defense? You *never* go to the range with me and can barely dismantle a Glock to clean. I'd rather be the one doing the shooting."

Just as Dom said it a woman with a child in her cart passed by, one of its wheels squeaking. Her eye was bruised and her daughter was crying silently. She stared at them before hurrying by. The levity they'd worked so hard for crashed and burned. Brian's smile faded and Dom turned his eyes to the floor.

But for every person who seemed off in the store, there were those who didn't seem to give a damn the city had riots breaking out. They blocked the aisles with their carts, chatting. A group of teenagers roamed the energy drink section, jostling each other and being obnoxious.

It was weird. Were they denying what was going on? Did they know? Or maybe they didn't care? He'd been in the same boat not a few days before, thinking it would all blow over.

Wait until they see it for themselves, Dom thought. *Then things will be different.*

As they piled Band-Aids and rubbing alcohol into the tops of their carts, Dom's phone rang. It was Chelsea. After what happened she slipped his mind. He hated himself for that.

Chelsea and Dom met years before at a mutual friend's party and were a match made in heaven. They both were movie buffs, frequenting the theater once or twice a week, and had an obsession with stouts and lagers. Deeper than that, despite their occasional fights and disagreements, they were always there for one another without being overbearing. Marriage was a possibility, one they had discussed, but Chelsea didn't want to until after she finished college.

"Hey, what's up?" Dom asked.

"Oh, end of the world. The usual."

Dom laughed. Brian made a face and a humping gesture, which sent Dom walking down the aisle away from him.

"Where are you?" she asked.

"The Fred Meyer in Mercer Island. You need anything?"

"I thought you were going to Wal-Mart?"

He swallowed the knot in his throat. "We did. It was kind of rough there."

"What does that mean?" Her voice lowered. "Did you get hurt? Is everything okay?"

"It's fine," he assured her. He passed the candy aisle. The same group of kids were shoving candy in their pockets and backpacks. A weary store clerk nearby saw them, but turned and walked away. "We're getting stuff here, then we'll come to get you. Sound good?"

"Yeah. Hey, Dom?"

"Hm?"

"Get some red vines, okay?"

He laughed. "One step ahead of you."

6 The Infected

Dan Rector wasn't sure why he had bad luck. He'd read a book about a guy who could poach luck, stealing it away from people to sell to the highest bidder. The idea was appealing because then it meant his bad luck wasn't a cosmic joke. It was more of a sad affliction.

But it didn't matter what he told himself because, for whatever reason, he had the worst luck and it was going to get him killed. Not in a metaphoric kind of way.

It was literally going to get him killed in a matter of moments.

He'd done what the news said, staying inside his house, far from the hazards of whatever sickness was going around. He locked the doors and windows, closed the curtains, and stayed in the middle of the house where people wouldn't see him from the outside. To keep himself occupied he went over the lines he had in Macbeth, telling himself that when everything blew over he'd be the only one who'd be ready for the play.

He savored the imaginary conversation in his head.

Dan, that was fabulous!

An absolute miracle. At least we have one true actor amongst us.

As he watched the news he even began to feel safe. The closest incident of infection was two cities away. He'd done a good job locking down the house. There wasn't much reason *to be* afraid. The media was probably blowing things out of proportion anyway. Sure, there was an inkling of fear. A nagging 'what if' in the back of his head. But he was sure everyone felt that way.

Then someone broke the backdoor window. Dan heard it, reacting slowly and going for the garage rather than the front door—a deadly mistake. Had he gone for the front door he might've been able to make a run for it. Yet all he thought was *get to the car*.

The woman who broke in was obviously one of the infected people. Her eyes were bloody and she stunk like sour milk and dumpsters. There was something in the way she whispered nonsense to herself, her limbs jerking of their own accord, which gave Dan a primal sense of fear he had known well as a child when his parents turned his bedroom light off.

He wanted to place her somewhere; maybe if he knew her it would explain why she picked *his* house out of *all* the houses. But deep down, Dan knew he'd never seen her before. It was luck. Bad, bad luck.

At gunpoint, she made Dan take his clothes off and tied him to the dining room table. The view of his kitchen ceiling wasn't familiar to him. He tried focusing on the dusty chandelier, taking ragged breaths in between begging her to leave.

Once he was tied up she stood back, setting the gun on the counter. "I'm a chef," she said. She laughed maniacally. Saliva dribbled down her chin. "I'm best known for my butcher...butcherrrring."

The words stumbled from her lips. She gnawed on her tongue until a sliver of blood mixed with the saliva on her chin, and spun around. She began jerking open drawers, silverware clattering loudly.

Dan's bad luck had made him particularly resilient in bad situations, but this was beyond such things. He felt the first sob building in his throat; when he saw the fillet knife she pulled from his knife block, the sob released in one long wail. His begging escalated.

"Please, don't. You don't have to do this."

PULSE

The crazy woman leaned over him, prodding his thigh, then his bicep. His hip. Wherever her mind was, it was miles away. She brought the tip of the knife to his bicep and ran it in one clean, smooth stroke. Blood gushed and searing pain coursed through his body. He wasn't sure what was louder; his screams or her laughs.

Another stroke of the knife, another. He felt weight lift from his arm and saw that it was because she'd removed the meat of his bicep. She hefted it in her hands and set it on the counter.

"Tasty. Tassssty. I'm a good butcher. With a buerre blanc this will be delighttfullll!"

Dan wasn't lucky. If he was, he would've fallen unconscious early on. Instead, he stayed awake as she sliced away at his other bicep and his forearms, flaying him alive.

31

7 Dom

Chelsea's apartment was in a forested area off the main highway. The ride was quick and peaceful. They'd gotten at least a hundred cans of food, a variety of medical supplies, and all the sweets they'd been lusting for. The cashier commented on how they'd made a smart move coming in when they did, because shipments were being canceled right and left.

"We have to get new deliveries every day to keep items in stock," he said. "You'd be surprised how fast we run out of stuff if even one shipment is canceled. It's going to be like Christmas, but ten times worse."

Despite Brian's ruthless teasing, Dom picked up a few boxes of condoms. If Chelsea was coming to stay for an indeterminate amount of time, they were bound to do something physical *eventually*. Having a baby during a zombie apocalypse wasn't the best survival move. He was being smart.

'Zombie.' Dom still wasn't sure if that was a word he should be using. He hadn't seen a zombie, hadn't seen someone that was definitely a zombie on TV. The real threat were the people murdering each other a thousand miles away in seemingly non-zombie related ways.

But when he reminded himself people were harming each other a few miles away at the mere prospect of the end of days, where no signs of the infection had even been reported, it made it all worse.

The news kept calling it 'infection' or 'the infectious disease.' The official world used those words, but everyone else was calling it 'zombies' or the 'zombie apocalypse'. It was no wonder it was in his head.

"Hey, we're here. You go get her, I'll stay in the car." Brian whipped out his phone. Dom caught a glimpse of the red and white CNN interface before hopping out.

The apartment complex was quiet, but not in an unsettling way. No signs of chaos here and Dom was glad for it. He hopped out of the car and began the walk up to her second story apartment. He didn't see her roommate's car in its spot and he was glad for that, too. In addition to a baby, the next to last thing he wanted was to spend more than an hour with Cindy. He wasn't sure why Chelsea lived with her. They were childhood friends, but from what Dom understood Cindy wasn't remotely the same as when they were children. That was Chelsea's problem; sometimes she was loyal to the point of harming herself.

She opened the door before he had to knock and wrapped her arms around him.

"I'm so happy to see you."

"I just talked to you on the phone," Dom said, trying to keep things light. "Of course I'm here."

She mumbled into his chest "I know. It's just scary. Been watching the news a lot, you know?"

Behind her he saw her shotgun in its case and two duffle bags. He pulled back to grin. He gave her a quick peck on the lips. "I guess it takes the apocalypse to get you to be ready on time?"

He saw the flicker of hesitation cross her face. Chelsea was very genuine and sweet, but sometimes gullible. He knew she was thinking about whether to flip out or laugh. She chose the latter and relief washed over him.

"I guess so," she said. "I have bad news though."

Dom walked past her to grab her stuff. "What?"

"Cindy took all the food and jumped ship."

"What?" He thought about it. Chelsea didn't have much in the way of supplies to begin with. It wasn't a loss and he didn't want to make the situation worse. She was obviously hurt. "Don't worry about it. We got a ton of stuff. Maybe we can stop at that little store on the way home. Sound good? And Brian's car can barely fit more than we have, so you're good."

She picked up her shotgun case, looking happy with herself. "It would make me feel better. I feel like I'm already dead weight. Plus I want to pick up some cough drops and Sudafed, I think I might be getting sick."

He clicked his tongue in mock disapproval. "I don't think you could've picked a worse time to be sick."

Chelsea rolled her eyes, changing the subject to how she couldn't believe what Cindy did. Dom supplied sympathetic noises on cue.

"Also, I was going to call work and take a few days off, but my manager called *me* first and said not to come in," she said. "Jonas has family in the mid-west so I guess he's trying to deal with that or something."

Chelsea worked in a family owned computer repair shop a few hours a week while she finished her nutrition degree. From what Dom gathered, it was a great place to work. Flexible hours, good people. He was envious.

"Anne let us take a day off. I don't work again until next week, but if things keep getting bad I bet a lot of places will start closing until further notice," Dom said.

"I don't know why you don't find another job." Chelsea shifted the shotgun to her other hand. "You hate everything about working there."

"I know, I know," he laughed. "I'm just complaining."

Brian was still glued to his phone when they got back to the car. He'd torn open a bag of Skittles which rested on Dom's side of the seat, a few rainbow candies scattered on the cushion and ground. Dom situated Chelsea's items in the trunk, cleaned off his seat and got in.

"Chelsea wants to stop at that small store we passed before we head home," Dom said.

Brian set his phone in the cup holder and craned his neck back to look at Chelsea. "You sure? With her in here we won't have much room for more stuff."

"Hey!" she snapped.

He shrugged. "Not a fat comment, Chels. Get ahold of yourself."

It *was* hard to wedge her in with all the clunky bags of food, but they managed. Dom saw no harm in grabbing more nonedible items like ibuprofen, cold medicine, and the like. Who knew when they'd have another chance to leave the house? While he didn't *want* to be isolated to his apartment, he had to acknowledge it was a possibility.

Brian navigated out of the apartment complex. Everyone braced themselves as they exited, going over a handful of speed bumps. All the canned goods clunked against each other, tumbling and resettling.

"Someone needs to stay in the car. We don't want to let this stuff sit around unsupervised," Brian said as they drove. "I volunteer as long as you keep things brief. No browsing the makeup or shampoo." He winked at Chelsea who gave him the finger.

"I'm not sure you could be any more sexist," she said under her breath.

Dom hit Brian on the shoulder and it ended the little tiff. If they were already at it now, things were only going to get worse. They didn't like each other in the way only the best friend and girlfriend can.

At best, they could tolerate each other. Asking for anything more would be unwise.

***

When the glass doors slid open, Dom knew something was up. There was a silence over the mom and pop grocery store that made his hair stand on end. They'd only taken a few steps when Dom spotted the man with a gun at the cash register. He pulled Chelsea aside, cursing himself for brushing against the chip bags and making them crinkle.

He didn't hear any response. The man hadn't heard.

"Give me all the money," the man shouted. "I know you have more back there!"

In broken English the clerk told him they didn't. They didn't carry more cash than what he gave him. They didn't have a safe.

He begged. Pleaded for his life.

Dom wasn't sure if the robber was hopped up on drugs or fear, but he wasn't taking no for an answer.

"Dom?" Chelsea's voice quavered.

He shushed her and took hold of her hand, giving it a reassuring squeeze. They could run out again, they'd walked in easily enough without anyone noticing. Couldn't they slip out again too? But anxiety was in the way. He wanted to be brave for Chelsea, but he wasn't sure he could, not when he couldn't make his own body move.

A shot echoed through the store.

Chelsea screamed. Dom thought he did, too. There were panicked shouts throughout the store. Footsteps pounded down the tile floor approaching them. The robber, now murderer, stood in front of them.

For the second time that day, Dom had a gun pointed at his head. The man was shaking just as much as they were. A smear of blood across the tops of his hands. There was more on the paper bag he clutched in them.

"You...you... stay back!" The man glanced around, then darted out the doors.

Dom thought that was the worst thing that could've happened. The cashier lost his life for a presumably petty amount of money. But as the murderer left the scene, hell broke loose in the store. All the people that had been in hiding burst into action.

Now that the cashier—the emblem of order—was gone, it was free game.

A woman pushed her cart down the aisle where they crouched, using her arm to sweep everything off the shelves into her basket. Bags of snacks and chips scattered onto the floor and burst as she rolled over them.

Dom found his legs and stood, dragging Chelsea with him. A few extra supplies wasn't worth risking their lives. They began moving towards the exit when Chelsea stopped him. "We need to get as much stuff as we can."

This was ridiculous. Chelsea was falling victim to the same feral sense that the rest of the store patrons were. Dom shook his head. "*No!* Listen to yourself, just because they're acting crazy and stealing doesn't mean we should."

To their right a middle aged woman shoved them aside, using the case of beer in her arms to knock them back. She was just clearing the exit when a man slammed into her. A verbal fight broke out. Things were going from bad to worse.

"We're leaving," Dom said. "Now."

He didn't wait for an answer. They made their way back to the exit. Dom caught sight of the cashier behind the counter. Blood splattered the cigarette case behind him and was pooling on the ground. A strong metallic tang hung heavy in the air. He veered Chelsea away so she wouldn't have to see, but he heard her gasp.

Brian had the car started before they even arrived. The second the doors closed he peeled out of the parking lot.

"Are you okay?"

"Yes."

"What happened? I heard a gunshot."

"Someone got shot."

"Fuck, are you serious?"

Dom heard Chelsea crying softly in the backseat. He glanced in the rearview mirror. Her cheeks were ruddy. She caught him looking and turned her head.

"Dom, are you serious?"

"For fuck's sake, I wouldn't say it if it weren't true!"

Brian's mouth snapped shut. They drove in silence until they were at the apartment complex. No further incidents delayed them and the streets were clear. The chaos and violence were sporadic. Dom imagined they were breaking out here and there, perhaps sparked by one crazy person with a gun and a mission, but at the rate they were going it was only a matter of time before it was every person for themselves.

And the infection wasn't even close yet. That's what made him the angriest. If people worked together—or at the very least stayed calm—none of this would be happening. The cashier's brains wouldn't be splattered on the cigarette case, Chelsea wouldn't be sobbing in the backseat, and Brian...

Well, Brian would still be Brian.

Dom slammed his fist against the dashboard, surprising even himself. They'd just pulled into a parking spot on the street. His friends stared at him with wide eyes.

"I'm sorry," he muttered. "It was a lot to take."

Brian nodded. He fiddled with his keys, looking anywhere but at Dom. "It's okay. It is. I'm sorry I was acting like a dick. Let's get all this stuff upstairs, have a beer, and forget it ever happened."

"That's the best plan I've heard all day," Dom said.

8 Price Family

Sam was worried about Lindsey, who had yet to wake up. He was more worried about Sally. The resonating anxiety was beyond anything he'd ever felt before. He tried to call 911, but he was redirected or put on hold. No doubt it had to do with the massacre at the hospital.

Lindsey left a voicemail on his phone. His jaw dropped as he listened to her explain what she'd seen, and that she was going to take Lindsey to the ER a town over. He sped all the way home, bursting in the door and running down the hallway. Lindsey was on the floor of Sally's room, unconscious. Sally was so sick, so unbelievably sick.

They needed to get to the hospital, but when he tried to move Sally she screamed in pain. He hated to admit it, but that wasn't the worst part. The smell of her sweat was so putrid, so acidic, it made Sam vomit when he came too close. It drove him from the room. He even put a blanket under the door to prevent it from entering the rest of the house.

Sally was his life, and there he was, so weak nerved that he couldn't stomach a bad smell to be with her. His only daughter—his world. Guilt and embarrassment ate away at him; a bad combination, one he knew led him to make bad decisions.

Was that what made Lindsey faint? The smell? The sight of their daughter in so much pain?

Sitting at the dining room table, he dialed 911 again. Then the hospital. The hospital across town. There was no response. Sam was never great at dealing with stress like this. Lindsey balanced them out that way. She always knew what to do, what to say, and how to do it. He glanced at the cupboard above the fridge. He needed a drink. Eight years sober was about to go down the drain.

He felt his face get hot. Why did they even *have* alcohol in the house? After everything he went through to get sober, it was downright offensive that Lindsey brought it into the house.

Sam caught himself and took a deep breath. It wasn't Lindsey's fault. This wasn't him. It was his bad side trying to get the best of him. He was just stressed.

Instead of wallowing, he set down the phone and went to see Lindsey. He'd laid her on the couch after she fainted. It had been almost an hour.

He held his breath as he passed his daughter's room.

"Sam?"

Lindsey called his name as he entered the living room. She was sitting up, staring at her hands, which quivered. Her face was white.

"Hey, babe," he whispered. He slid next to her, setting his arm around her shoulders. "Are you okay?"

"Something is wrong with Sally."

"Yeah, I tried calling the hospital but—"

"No. Something is *wrong* with her. Seriously *wrong*," she said, louder this time.

Sam's brow furrowed. Something was wrong with Lindsey, too. "What?"

"There's something in her stomach. I saw it before I fainted." She glanced at the hallway, then to Sam. Her eyes were distant.

A chill ran down his spine. She wasn't lying. Whatever she thought she saw, she believed it. "How's this? I'll go check on her. We'll get her in the car and drive to a hospital. We don't leave until they let us in, okay?"

Barely a nod, but it was a yes. She insisted she went with him, despite his protests.

Sam and Lindsey went to their daughter's room. As he set his hand on the doorknob he heard her first wail.

"Mommy?"

Sam looked at his wife. Their little girl's voice was ragged, yet...taunting.

"Daddy?"

As Sam opened the door and saw the first of the white, squirming creatures on the floor, he regretted not having that last drink.

Eloise J. Knapp

9 Dom

It took five trips to haul everything up to the apartment. By the end of it their hands were bright red with indents from where the heavy bags pressed. They'd all broken out into a sweat and were breathless. Chelsea tripped on the stairs and banged up her knee. Dom's biceps and shoulders throbbed.

But their haul was immense and it was grins all around. They had enough food to last them another three months with moderate rations. Some of it required more cooking and effort, but it was doable. Brian tore open some licorice and they took a sugar break before their next move.

"I guess we should organize this into the spare room, right?" Chelsea ate her candy slowly. Her pouty lips were stained red. "It's important not to let things get disorderly during a survival scenario."

"You been watching Doomsday Preppers?" Brian asked.

She laughed. "You guessed it. Most of my survival knowledge comes from that show."

"It's a good show."

Brian and Chelsea shared a brief moment of camaraderie, giving Dom a flicker of hope.

They heard pounding and shouting from the hallway. Luggage rolling against the floor. Everyone sat a little taller, alert, listening. Then it was silent. Dom shrugged.

"Maybe after we organize everything we should write down an inventory?" Chelsea rubbed at her knees, staring pensively out the window. "That way we can go by numbers instead of just guessing how much stuff we have."

42

"I second that," Brian added. "We should fortify the apartment, too."

"Should we try to ally with neighbors? And how much ammo do we have?"

"Come on you guys. Things got a little weird today but we shouldn't overreact." Dom knew he was being a killjoy but someone had to bring them down to earth. "Isn't that something survivalists value? Not overreacting and exacerbating?"

The looks Brian and Chelsea gave him shut him up. He was about to get irritated but the two laughed. "We're just screwing around. But the inventory thing is a good idea," Chelsea said.

After their break they started arranging their supplies in the spare room. Dom wished they had shelves to make things look neater and be more accessible, but he wasn't about to go to the store again. Some of the can piles reached as high as his waist.

It made him think of his mom. He hadn't called her to make sure she was okay. He hadn't thought it was necessary, what with being so far away from the infection. They never had a close relationship, but if there was any time it was now. He made a note to give her a call that night, after they were settled.

They moved food that was expired, or ready to expire, to the kitchen so they could eat it first. The rest of their food that was ready to eat, like soup, chili, and precooked dinners, went into one quarter of the room. Veggies and broths went into their own corner, then meats and miscellaneous next to them. Dry goods had a section on their own. They gutted the linen closet—that's what Chelsea called it—and put all the medical supplies in it.

It was Chelsea's idea to keep the food organized like a grocery store so when they went to make food, the goods would be easy to find. That led to Dom and Brian voting her official Apocalypse Cook, a title which she gladly accepted since she liked cooking anyway.

Brian managed to refrain from making jokes about a woman in the kitchen. Things were shaping up.

"Plus, I doubt you guys could cook anything worth eating," she joked. "I'd rather not risk it."

It took a few hours but eventually they had a well-organized inventory of supplies. It was satisfying to see it all, and Dom knew his mom would be proud.

He insisted they pack bug-out bags for each of them to keep at the door just in case. Another thing his mom taught him long before TV became obsessed with it. Enough food and water for two days, plus other necessary supplies. The hard reality was that, if they ever needed to bug-out, the weight of the packs would slow them down. None of them were accustomed to carrying much weight for a long duration of time. Dom hoped it wouldn't come to that.

By the time they were done they were ravenous. Chelsea wanted to use up what few fresh ingredients they had in the fridge to make a stew and cheese bread. The apartment smelled amazing and for a moment life was ordinary. Brian was zoned out on the TV and barely posed a threat as a third wheel. Chelsea's hips swayed as she stirred something on the stove, and Dom was happy to be there.

Then the shouting started. They all held their breath listening. Someone, a woman, was sobbing.

"Please Brett, please don't shoot me!"

Dom was at the door in a heartbeat. Through the peephole he saw his neighbors, Brett and Sadie, and their toddler son outside their apartment door. Sadie was hunched over, back against the wall, clutching a bleeding nose. Her son was standing in shock, unsure of what to do. Tears streamed down his round cheeks.

"You thought you'd just leave?"

"It's dangerous here, there are fights and I...I just wanted to protect Jon."

Dom spotted the revolver in Brett's hand. He'd called the police for domestic violence before. Brett hit Sadie on more than a few occasions. They were separated, but when he got drunk he'd come and beat on them. Sadie's cousin would come and take the son for weeks on end.

"Don't get involved," came Brian's voice in a whisper.

Dom hadn't even realized his hand was on the doorknob.

"It'll work itself out," Brian said. "It usually does."

From the kitchen, Chelsea's face was white. She and her mother were physically abused by her father up until the second they walked out. Whenever they saw the slightest sign of domestic violence, Chelsea clammed up or got angry and was the good Samaritan some people could only dream of being.

Chelsea's past aside, Dom wasn't going to let this go. He'd called before, but this time was serious. Brett never had a gun before. It could affect them, too.

He opened the door. Three faces turned and gaped at him.

"Listen 408, you don't have nothing to see here. Now get," Brett said.

Dom shook his head. "I think you need to go. Sadie?"

Sadie had the same look on her face she always did when Dom tried to step in before. She was grateful, but afraid to speak up for herself or agree. Usually she wavered in a limbo state waiting for one of them to make the next move.

"You need to go, Brett."

But this time was different.

"Bitch, I'm not going anywhere! You fu—"

The distinct sound of a shell being chambered into a shotgun cut his profanity short. Dom turned to see Chelsea standing behind him with a shotgun, aimed straight for Brett's head. Brett began raising the gun in his hand when Chelsea took a step forward.

"Put down the gun." Her voice was steady. "Sadie, take it. Brett, you get out of here. If I see you again, you're dead."

He did as she said. His face was bright red, veins bulging in his forehead and neck. Before he started down the stairs he shot Sadie a menacing glare. But once he was gone everyone's shoulders loosened and a tangible sensation of relief washed over them.

"Thank you," Sadie said, getting to her feet and taking her son by the hand. "I tried to leave earlier with Jon, get away you know? Then he showed up as I was going to my cousin's house and dragged us back up here."

Chelsea set the shotgun against the doorframe. "It's fine. Don't let him tell you who's boss." She picked up the handgun Brett left and handed it to her. "*You're* the boss now, got it?"

Vigorous nodding. "I'm the boss."

They exchanged goodbyes and shut the door. This was a side of Chelsea Dom hadn't seen before, but it was reassuring. Maybe a bit scary, but it made him love her even more.

"I'll finish up dinner. Five minutes then we'll eat."

The guys nodded, and just like that the incident was over. Like the Wal-Mart and dead cashier, it was another scene to add to the growing bank of memories they all wanted to forget.

10 Adam

"What am I looking at? Ascaris or something?"

Barry, his primary lab guru, nodded and shrugged at the same time. It was an odd gesture that didn't confirm or deny. "Looks like working in an office hasn't dulled your senses, but not quite. It's a parasitic nematode, so you're right there. At first I thought it was a roundworm, but it's actually of the genus Anisakis. The difference is that Ascaris lives in the intestines, whereas Anisakis can exist not only on the *outside* of organs, but in muscle and under the skin."

Adam racked his brain, looking back to a seminar he attended on parasitic infections for anything he could remember on Anisakis. "If I recall correctly, it sounds like a scary parasite but it can't live in the host for very long. Neither can its larvae."

"Mhm, all true. But, although this looks like, and preliminary tests showed similar genetics to, it isn't Anisakis," Barry said.

"Thanks for the fun lecture, but why am I looking at it? You know highest priority is identifying the virus in the North Dakota patients."

"That *is* why you're looking at it. This is it. I'm calling it *Anisakis Nova*."

The name made it sound impressive, but at the end of the day it just meant 'new Anisakis' which didn't mean much. Barry had a way of fancying things up. That thought was fleeting compared to the reality of what he just said. They were finding parasites in the bodies. Not a virus, but parasites.

Adam shifted, getting a better look through the microscope. The worm-like figure wiggled. He magnified it further and noted the jagged teeth of its perfectly round mouth. He didn't want to get ahead of himself, which was why the following question was out of hope more than anything else. "So this one victim happened to have a parasite and the virus. People eat raw or improperly handled fish all the time. Hell, no one should even *be* eating sushi in North Dakota."

He seemed to sense what Adam was going for. "Sorry, buddy. We've found Anisakis Nova in every sample sent so far. Some are in larvae stage, some bigger. But they're there."

Adam caved. "Prelim tests showed similar genetics, but what?"

"But there's sequencing in here that is way too complicated for a simple parasite, and definitely not related to Anisakis." Barry spread pages of analysis on the desk in front of them, but Adam couldn't take his eyes off the parasite. "Here's the deal: we left it in a dish of human blood to see how it would react. Did a before and after analysis on the blood. It's using whatever host materials it has to synthesize a chemical compound that causes a response similar to encephalitis."

"Encephalitis?" Adam repeated.

"Acute inflammation of the brain."

He rolled his eyes but couldn't help but grin in good nature. "I know what it is, Barry."

"Just keeping you in check, big man," he said, returning the smile. He leaned back in his chair. "You're looking at fever, confusion, and headaches early on. Once it gets worse, a whole onslaught of physical and neurological problems. Hallucinations are common. Seizures, tremors. Memory loss, I think."

"You said it uses host materials. Does that mean it isn't synthesizing now?"

Barry nodded. "Right. As soon as you put it in the blood of a mammal it starts production. And *fast*. When removed from a source of sustenance it simply stops production and keeps on living."

"How long can it last on its own like this?"

"This one has been without a host since we extracted it from one of the hospital bodies."

Adam felt his blood go cold. "It can live on a slide for a week?"

"So far. It doesn't seem to show any signs of decay."

It was a hyper aggressive parasite that was essentially foreign to his team, made people kill each other, and could live outside of any food source for a week. How was that possible?

"God, what a nightmare," Adam groaned. He gestured to the chemical analysis. "Those for me?"

"Take them. I practically have them memorized by now."

Adam straightened the stack. "Keep at it. Whatever you need to continue analysis on these, you got it. We need everyone on this. Find as much information as you can on parasites that cause such erratic behavior and violence, and any other related viruses, diseases, or parasites. We need everything we can get our hands on."

"You got it."

***

Adam was fascinated by the parasite. It was highly adaptive, unlike anything he'd ever seen. He had no data on the first victim, Jay Lehmann, but based on what he'd learned from the grocery store victims and the most recent reports (which were always sparse and not nearly as

49

detailed as he'd like), and the help of the lab geeks and his favorite epidemiologist, he was able to put together a timeline on infection rate.

Stage one was initial contact. It seemed as though any bodily fluid transfer would infect, meaning the organism was microscopic and could enter the body with ease. Bites and scratches were the most effective way the hosts transferred it, but any contact with it would do. Since it could live outside of the body for an indeterminate length of time, hypothetically any area a host was in contact with could harbor it.

It was much more sophisticated than the traditional parasitic worm model, which was for the host to ingest the worm, cough up eggs, swallow them, and then it grew in their intestines or other parts of the body. In this case the parasite seems to exist in all parts of the body; every tissue and blood sample thus far had yielded at least a handful of the little buggers.

Stage two was illness. The nausea, bursting capillaries in eyes, fever, and sweat. Adam believed this was the period of time the body was attempting to fight it, but it was too strong. It dominated the human immune system, took over like a plague.

Stage three was the coma. At this point the body is no longer able to stay conscious as it infects the entire body. The autopsy results revealed the parasites primarily conglomerated in the chest cavity, but often they were found clustered around the base of the neck and in the brain.

Stage four was, for lack of better words, complete insanity. The victims awoke violent, mentally disturbed, and with no trace of their former selves. It was like Barry said—encephalitis—but mixed with rabies and a bad acid trip.

Adam finished typing the last words of his report to send to the higher-ups. He knew the technicalities, the stages, the methods. Now it felt like a waiting game to see how bad it could get and how fast they could find a solution. He felt a little better having written down the stages and analyzed some data of his own. It felt right to him.

But really, it was all grim, but with their new solid information things were looking up.

Facts, he told himself. *We're getting the facts.*

Another email popped up in his inbox. It was an apology from Jon Sanders, a guy who sent a tasteless email earlier. Jon sent it to the entire CDC; a picture of a zombie from a popular TV show. Adam could barely remember the words underneath it, but it was outrageously offensive. In retrospect, the behavior the infected exhibited was an awful like what movies showed, but the joke was still inappropriate. He hoped Jon was punished severely for it.

His phone rang. He checked the caller ID. It was his direct contact field agent, Erik Eskilson.

"This is Baker," he said. "Erik, tell me something good."

There was commotion on the other end. "It's worse."

Adam's blood pressure skyrocketed. "What do you mean?"

"The parasite evolved. It's growing."

"I know; the infection rate is spreading quickly. That isn't something to be so dramatic about—"

"No, Adam. It's *growing*. The parasite is physically growing in size. I'm sending photos now. I've gotta go, I'll call you as soon as I know more."

Erik hung up. Adam tabbed out of his report to his email. Moments later a new message popped up with a zipped file. There were five images, each worse than the last.

As he stared at the bloody, gaping hole in a little girl's chest cavity, he felt his lunch threaten to come up.

This *was* worse. Much worse.

11 The Infected

The Missoula emergency room was packed beyond sanitary capacity. Every bed was filled, some with more than one person, and the remainders were slumped against walls and piled on top of each other. The sounds of moaning and crying merged into a constant hum of depression and sorrow. Only the occasional shrill scream broke the sick from their daze.

Craig Scott was one of the few nurses who hadn't jumped ship when things got bad, but now he was regretting it. As he made his way down the hall, stepping over and around the overflow of patients, he knew there was nothing anyone could do for the infected. They had no vaccine, no method of treating it. They didn't even have a way of giving comfort in the smallest of ways. No spare blankets, no food. No nurses or volunteers to hold hands and say everything would be okay.

He paused in front of the maternity ward entrance. It, too, was overrun with the town's infected. It was the last to go, since all the doctors did their best to keep that area free from potential infection. Eventually there was no choice. Some of the women were taken home, others with more sensitive situations airlifted to another hospital. Instead, the most severe cases were kept—no, *stored*—in there. If they weren't in the feverish, flu-like stage, they were in a coma.

But how long until his hospital was overrun, too? And when they woke up?

Craig and the other nurses felt the impending destruction. As soon as the comatose patients awoke, they would be violent. The entire hospital was aware of the circumstances, yet many still wanted to help and see it through. Craig was one of them.

"Nurse, please, can I get some water?"

Sitting on the ground was a young woman. Her damp hair clung to her face. The foul sweat all the infected had was just beginning to manifest on her pale skin. The ice blue shade of her irises against the reddening whites was unsettling.

She had her hand on Craig's leg. It took everything he had not to shake it off.

"Sure," Craig said, his voice muffled through the respirator all the staff took to wearing. "I'll get you some."

By the time he got back, the girl would probably be in the coma.

Somewhere down the hall came another scream. A scuffle.

A gunshot.

A hush went down the hallway. Another two shots were fired and the entire hospital went into a frenzy. The wave of panic was instantaneous. Anyone who could walk was up and fleeing. They trampled those who were disabled.

Craig was shoved aside. His back hit the maternity ward doors, then they swung open. He fell flat on his back, catching sight of the mass of infected moving past before they swung shut.

"Help me."

He turned. A man lay under a gurney. Two children were huddled around him. He looked at Craig with a desperation so pure it made his heart ache.

"I'm sorry," he mumbled as he got up. "I'm sorry, there's nothing I can do"

There was no movement in the maternity ward because everyone in it was unconscious. Bodies were packed like sardines in beds, cots, and sheets on the ground. There were quadruple the amount since the last time he'd been in there.

There were no doctors or nurses in sight. Just people left to die. To his right he saw movement. Some of the infected began convulsing. Their limbs twitched erratically, hitting the nearest bodies next to them with loud thuds. One rolled off his bed onto two other people who began moving, too.

Craig tried to remember the protocol notes they were given when the infection first reached Missoula. Somewhere in it, it said to restrain victims who showed signs of consciousness when emerging from the coma. There was no way to restrain this many people.

Fear coursed through him. Thirty feet away a woman stood, her body hunched over, hands forming claws by her side. Her chest heaved. She looked straight at Craig.

He turned to escape, but one of the risen infected blocked his way. It was a man old enough to be his grandfather. His red eyes bore into Craig. Spittle flew from his mouth as he growled and lunged. He grabbed a hold of Craig's I.D badge, tearing it from his neck as he jumped back.

Then the smell hit him with such voraciousness that he couldn't stop the spew of vomit. It caught in his mask, choking him. He ripped it off and fell to his knees. He felt dizzy. He tasted the smell, the acrid, thick scent of infected sweat.

The old man was on him. The others were rising, howling and grunting with the need to destroy. He watched in horror as they swarmed him, all fists and mouths. He screamed as they tore him apart, piece by piece, until he couldn't anymore.

12 Dom

Laying in Dom's bed, he and Chelsea watched TV late into the night. A few channels were taken over by broadcasts about the infection. No good news. It made the afterglow of their dinner—spaghetti with vegetables—fade fast.

"The infection has spread, its reach now extending to the edges of Montana. We have reports of mass groups of infected individuals moving in all directions across the state."

The scene cut from a pretty blonde news anchor to blurry cell footage of a crowded mall. It was dark. The sound was muted, but Dom could imagine the screaming. The smell of blood. Some figures were obviously aggressors, but since everyone was running it was hard to tell.

The blonde's "expert guest" piped up. "Debra, we've also noticed many social media networks are crashing due to overwhelming amounts of activity. People are quick to upload videos and photos to the internet. This is likely what's causing widespread panic across the nation, even in uninfected regions."

"Are you saying people are still managing to get off a tweet before they die?" Her tone was short. The comment wasn't from her teleprompter, based on the hard glare she was giving the man.

The shot cut away from the expert, who looked very haggard and very interested in telling the truth, to a close-up of the blonde. When it cut back out the man was gone.

Dom felt sick. Was the man telling more than he should've and they yanked him off air? Were the news channels trying to keep things quiet?

"Still no word from the CDC or any other government officials on what course of action citizens should be taking," the lady said, her eyes glazing over as she read from the teleprompter. "We're still left with the words from the CDC earlier this week on quarantine and staying calm. Now, let's take a look at the latest exploits of our three favorite sisters."

Chelsea huffed and grabbed the remote. "Stay calm? What a joke. Go to KOMO. Let's see what the local news is saying. Maybe they aren't pulling people off the air."

KOMO didn't have any perspective on the nation-wide infection. Instead they were covering the mass chaos erupting over Washington state. Widespread panic was causing major traffic problems as people decided to pick up and flee to the ocean or the mountains. Panning shots of I90, 405, and Highway 2 showed bumper to bumper backup, some people abandoning their cars to make it on foot.

The news anchor commented on how startling it was that people were already desperate and harming each other.

The next series of clips were of different chain stores in bad repair. One was even the Wal-Mart they'd been to the previous day. Dom saw the same car, now burned to a skeleton of metal. After the montage, the news anchor launched into advice people should follow to stay safe. Nothing they hadn't heard before.

Sighing again, Chelsea slung her forearm over her eyes. "I'm not sure I can watch more news."

Dom was in agreement. Lately it felt like there was nothing else to do *but* watch the news, only it soured everyone's mood. He started flicking channels, searching for reruns or movies to watch. At last he found a comedy focusing around retail workers. It reminded him of regular life, before the infection, before all the craziness.

"It's going to be weird when we go back to work after all this," Dom said. He imagined Anne and making pretentiously complicated coffee drinks. Not something to look forward to.

Chelsea started laughing. "God, I know! The last lady I helped brought a tablet in because it wouldn't hold a charge. She didn't bring the power cord, so I told her she needed to go home and get it."

"I'm sure she was happy about that." Chelsea's work stories were always the same—most retail rage was—but she always told them with so much energy and hatred, Dom found it adorable and listened without complaint.

"Oh, yeah. She did come back with the cord and I plugged it in and, behold, it turned right on. She claimed it was a fluke and it wouldn't stay charged. I said she'd need to leave it so I could recharge it and let it run a few hours." Chelsea tapped the palm of her hand against Dom's chest to emphasize certain words in her story. "She said, 'No! I don't want to wait.' It's like, what do you want me to do, lady? Wave a magic wand and fix it?"

"Is that what you told her?"

"Of course. Then I slapped her in the face and told her to go elsewhere."

That was the big joke between them; customer service reps should be able to slap mean customers to put them in their place. It was ridiculous, but they found it hilarious.

"I punched a few people last week myself. Showed those customers who is boss," Dom said, puffing his chest out.

"You did, huh?" Chelsea maneuvered herself over him, throwing one leg over his body to straddle him. She bent down and planted a gentle kiss on his neck. "My champion."

Dom's pulse quickened. His hands moved up to her hips. "Do I get an award for my heroic actions?"

She nodded and dipped down again, showering his cheeks and forehead with kisses, her fingertips running along his jaw and down his neck. She pulled back, her expression gentle and focused entirely on him.

"I love you," she whispered.

"I love you too," he told her, meaning it more than words could ever express.

13 Adam

Barry got spooked and jumped ship. No one had heard from him for a day, but they didn't need to. He left a message with HR saying he was taking off an indefinite amount of time to be with his family. He wasn't the only one; a staggering 28% of staff took unpaid, personal time off, risking their jobs and any potential parting benefits.

Now Adam was left with Chandler, a slightly less intelligent version of Barry. He needed someone to harp on, someone to give him answers. Since Barry left, Adam felt like his lab work wasn't in good hands. He was forlorn that most of his own work involved paperwork, statements, and meetings. It made him feel rusty when it came to getting stuff done. The stages he'd come up with made sense, but some of it was speculation.

"Can you explain this to me?" Adam slapped the stack of photos down on Chandler's desk. His skin turned green as he looked away.

"Can *you* be a little more sensitive? Those pictures are horrific."

Adam rolled his eyes. "Don't you think I know that? This little girl *exploded*. Her chest cavity is *gone*." He leafed through the pictures, pulling out a close-up of a white worm-like creature five inches long. It was squashed in the middle like someone stepped on it.

"This. What is this? How is it so big and why aren't our samples this size?"

Chandler pursed his lips and stood from his desk, walking to various microscopes as though checking to make sure they hadn't grown. "I...I'm not sure, Dr. Baker.

None of our samples have increased or decreased in size. We measure them twice a day."

"Are you saying this didn't happen?" He waved the photo at Chandler. "We need to figure this out."

"We need a sample. We can't do anything but hypothesize without tissue samples of the parasite, blood samples from the host...God, this isn't TV. We don't have montages and then groundbreaking results after a day."

"Hypothesize, then. We haven't gotten a new infected sample recently. Is it possible it could've mutated that much in the space of what, a day?"

Another lab geek stepped forward. Apparently the whole lab was listening in. Adam had been yelling though, he should've expected it.

"Dr. Baker?"

"Speak. Go, tell me whatever you've got."

She wrung her hands together. "It seems obvious the parasite undergoes mutations in every generation, or perhaps every other generation. For example, if I infect you, you might not have a mutated form of the parasite. But when you infect Chandler, maybe it will mutate."

"That seems too random," Chandler snapped. "Why would it skip a generation? It makes more sense it would mutate every generation."

The girl—Dr. Marla Ainsworth, now that he looked at her badge—was unimpressed. "Genetic changes happen over time, Chandler. Ever heard of evolution? Anyway, parasites are relatively simple organisms. Their life cycle is rapid, allowing them faster mutation. Picture this." Her eyes sparkled and she used her hands making gestures with her explanation. "You've got patient zero, right? He infects two unrelated individuals, A and B. Stage three happens, during which the parasite either mutates or stays the same. A passes on the parasite to someone else, but based on how the parasite adapted to that specific body, no genetic changes occur. But when B gets infected, that same parasite experiences a new environment that changes it. Thus when B transmits to a new host, a *new version* of the parasite is being transferred. That's how it's random. A hundred parasites fathered from individual A might stay the same. It's chance."

A tech with a huge black beard and round glasses added, "That would easily explain why incubation times vary so dramatically. We're still getting reports of 4 day incubation times to 1 day."

"So you're telling me we have no way to predict how bad this thing will get or how fast it will spread." Adam ground his teeth, his eyes bearing down on Marla. "You're telling me mutation is entirely random."

"Unfortunately, yes. That's how it seems."

"Evolution takes thousands of years, millions! What you're saying, it just isn't conceivable."

Silence washed over the lab. People fidgeted and looked everywhere but at Adam. They weren't the ones who had to report this to the government. They weren't the ones making official statements to the entire country. They were basking in theories and the heat of a new biological discovery. Adam envied them.

Marla spoke up. "Dr. Baker, if we could just get live hosts we could observe, we might learn a lot more. We can't change the mutation factor, but with live hosts we could study the stages of infection in real time instead of going off the hospital and grocery store incident. Even the police and hospital reports we get now are never helpful. They say the same things over and over, none of it in scientific terms we might find helpful."

Glasses added, "And we're getting the sense they're so overwhelmed with what's happening, no amount of requesting or harping will get them to give us more."

Live hosts. They were almost *two thousand* miles away from live hosts. All the bodies they had were long since dead. But they had parasites; what if they just infected someone? It was corrupt, but desperate times...

His cell rang. He motioned the techs away and the unethical thoughts with them. It was Erik. "More bad news?"

"Not this time. Well, not for you at least. The little girl's parents are infected. We had them in questioning for 4 hours when both of them started experiencing Stage 2 symptoms."

Adam couldn't help but feel pride that everyone was adapting the stages from the report he filed. That moment of pride gave way to excitement once he realized what Erik said.

"And?"

"They're en route to you. They volunteered before they passed out."

Adam got the rest of the details from Erik and hung up. He looked at Marla who'd been honing in on the conversation. "It looks like your wish just came true."

14 Dr. Marla Ainsworth

Marla dropped her backpack in the hallway and headed straight for the kitchen. She was ravenous. The Indian takeout smelled divine and would be the perfect thing to soothe her nerves after the day she'd had at work.

Doom, her sassy tabby cat, jumped up on the counter as she pulled out the curry and naan, whining to the heaven's for a can of cat food. Marla obliged, letting the fat cat eat his food on the kitchen counter before returning to her own dinner.

She was both angry and pleased. Angry on count of Chandler, that chauvinistic jackass, trying to put her down and discredit her theories. Theories were important. If they didn't try thinking outside of the box, they'd never come up with answers. Everyone was wrapped up in the what, not the why.

Men were always like that. Too busy in their macho arrogance to get any real work done.

Marla hated confrontation—single crazy cat lady living in a studio apartment said it all—and usually would've stopped pushing her ideas right when Chandler started giving her a hard time. She didn't want to be the center of negative attention and often became flustered when she needed to defend herself.

But not this time, she thought triumphantly as she swirled her naan bread in the curry.

She knew she could hold her own intellectually against the other guys in the lab. It was only a matter of standing up for herself verbally. And today she had. Dr. Baker acknowledged her idea as valid, and everyone else did, too.

It was a triumph.

Marla moved her takeout boxes to the coffee table in front of her TV, gathering up the files she'd taken from work. She spread them out on the table and couch, settling in for an evening of research.

Tomorrow they'd have the Price couple. Live specimens infected with *Anisakis Nova*. She jotted down an outline of the tests they'd be able to do with live hosts, eating bites of takeout between. It was too soon to mention her ideas to anyone, but Marla suspected she might have an idea for a cure. It was just a thought, one she'd need to solidify before presenting to anyone.

Today *was* a victory, but she had to be careful around the lab being a semi-attractive (phrase coined by herself) woman. The guys were hard on her because they were intimidated. Even when she was right, they were quick to claim someone helped her, or that her success was by mere chance. It was childish and irritating, resulting in many nights of takeout accompanied by a few glasses of wine. Marla loved what she did, but often hated the people she worked with.

It was the same old story, really. She never wasted her breath complaining about it to the few friends she did have, because she knew most women suffered that type of discrimination. She figured the best way to combat it was to work hard to prove the naysayers wrong.

Her father always chastised her for going into science, claiming she brought upon herself the difficulties she experienced in work and throughout college. Her mother tried endlessly to support her, but being uneducated and having been a housewife almost her entire life, Marla never felt like her mother could truly relate to her. She loved her parents to death, and they loved her, but they were set in their old ways. Being an only child, she was on her own. Perhaps that was what made her so self-motivated; she wanted to prove to *herself* how far she could go, how much she could succeed. No external influences.

Marla finished off the takeout. Her stomach full, she was finally starting to relax. Doom, having finished his dinner and in need of attention, spread himself out across her papers on the couch. She pet him absentmindedly as she let her mind circulate around the parasite.

It was frightening. It was exciting. It was a jumble of things that made her very nervous. Working on an event like this was the kind of thing that would get her name into the history books forever, *especially* if she managed to find a cure or provide some relevant breakthrough. Yet the destruction it was causing brought her to one morbid thought: what if there was no world to write her into the books once it was all said and done?

God, what if she *did* find a cure, but no one in the pharmaceutical industry was alive to manufacture it?

Marla shuddered. It was an ugly, depressing thought. This was the makings of a horror movie.

She and many of the other scientists were in an odd position of experiencing both giddy fascination and complete terror that the infection would hit them. Before he left, Barry made a smart comment that started a fight in the lab.

"What magazines do you think will feature my work? It *is* the breakthrough kind of thing that gets a guy noticed. I should probably see a stylist now—"

Barry was cut off by Suresh. "Are you fucking kidding me? There are literally *thousands* of people dying every day, and you're worried about that shit?"

"I'm just trying to lighten the mood and—"

Suresh didn't let it go. "You're all living in la-la land. It's fun and cool to be in here, far away from anything that could hurt us, running tests on things that don't actually affect us. But it will soon and you'll be sorry."

The conversation ended there, Barry put in his place and fuming silently. She'd never admit it to anyone, but she was one of the la-la land people Suresh hated.

If there was one person who wasn't clueless or in denial, it was Dr. Baker. She didn't envy him, having to tell so many people so much bad news. He might not be doing work in the lab, but he was in the thick of things. Normally he was very put together, with his hair neatly gelled back and his clothes impeccably ironed. As the days wore on he became increasingly frazzled.

No one in the lab had an easy job—except Barry who decided he couldn't cut it, probably because of the fight with Suresh—but some parts of lab work was easier than that representative, red tape and fancy word junk.

Marla sighed. Break time was over. She retrieved her laptop and got to work.

15 The Infected

Taylor and Kyle passed a bottle of bad whiskey back and forth, their thighs and bottoms growing cold from the log they sat on. Katie and Brock made out in the backseat of Kyle's car just behind them. It was their official end-of-the-world party and so far it hadn't gone how Taylor hoped.

Kyle was helplessly in love with Katie, while Taylor was helplessly in love with him. Brock was just happy to have someone to bone. The whiskey she stole from her dad's stash helped, but didn't sooth the burn completely.

Overhead the moon was almost full. She stared at it in her liquor-induced state and wished for Kyle to make a move on her, too. Instead he sat, staring into the forest beyond the campfire. Taylor inched towards him, making sure her leg brushed up against his, and followed every tip Cosmo ever offered a girl for hooking up. None of it worked.

But the whole thing was an excuse to get together and do things she'd get grounded for, so even if she didn't hook up with Kyle she still got to drink and maybe smoke some weed. Mildred, Montana was close to North Dakota, but so in the middle of nowhere that she doubted the virus would get there. Nevertheless, they brought a baseball bat and machete and joked about killing some zombies, feeling like a bunch of badasses. She couldn't wait to tell Natasha about it at school.

They aren't zombies, her little sister said. *They are sick people!*

Taylor rolled her eyes and left for the night, climbing out of her bedroom window. They were zombies and it was the apocalypse. Plain and simple. It was cool.

"Hey, did you hear that?"

Kyle pushed himself off the log they sat on and took a few steps forward.

"I didn't hear anything."

"Listen."

Down the slope ahead of them she heard twigs cracking, but that wasn't anything unusual. They were in the forest a few miles outside of town; there were bound to be animals.

He picked up the baseball bat they'd painted the words *Zombie Killer* on and said, "Go get Brock."

Taylor got up but only took a few steps towards the car. "I don't want to," she whined. "Not when they're all over each other." They had the windows rolled down. She could hear them going at it.

"I just heard it again. Taylor you—"

Two people came running up the slope. She couldn't believe how fast they moved. Their bodies and eyes glinted in the campfire as they closed the distance between them, like they were wet. She thought they were pregnant women until she noticed the close cropped hair and realized they were men with huge bellies.

"Run! Run to the car!"

A spike of adrenaline coursed through Taylor's veins. They spun and made a dash towards the car. Taylor took one glance behind her and saw another handful of people— *zombies*—run into the firelight. These ones didn't have the big stomachs.

Kyle tripped behind her. She heard him go down but didn't turn back.

"Wait, help me!" he yelled.

She made it to the car and jerked the passenger door open. Brock was frantically trying to start the car, but it wouldn't go.

"I can't drive a clutch!" he said over and over. "I don't know what to do!"

The car made a series of clunking noises as he turned the key.

Taylor looked out the window. Some of the regular zombies were on Kyle, beating him and biting him. The rest were almost on the car.

Katie was in the backseat, half naked and sobbing as she groped around for her clothes. Brock abandoned trying to start the car and was halfway out the door. Taylor wished things had gone differently.

The rest of the zombies were finally at the car. The normal ones went straight for Brock, but the two pregnant looking ones shoved their stomachs through the windows.

One of them was laughing, singing the words to Ring Around the Rosies, his voice gleeful.

She closed her eyes as their stomachs exploded, launching thousands of worms into the car.

***

When Taylor went home, it wasn't to give her mom a hug and tell her she was okay. It wasn't to report the deaths of Katie or Kyle or Brock.

It was to kill her family.

The second she woke up in the front seat of Kyle's car, covered in blood and ooze, holes all over her body where the worms burrowed into her, she wanted to kill her family. Really, she always had. They cramped her style, never let her do what she wanted. It's just that now she could see clearly. Now there weren't any feelings stopping her from doing what she really wanted.

Her legs were stiff. She found her hands convulsing, head twitching to the right every time her left foot hit the ground. It was hard to walk. She wondered what was wrong with her, but the sensation was fleeting.

Kill   mom.   Kill   dad.   Kill   Libby. Killmomkilldadkilllibby.

Her mantra was at full blast in her mind. Soon it blocked any rational thoughts she might've had left after waking up.

The hardwood of her porch slapped against her bare feet. Taylor heard her parents yelling her name as they came to let her in.

Killmomkilldadkilllibby.

They couldn't stop her. When she ripped mom's throat out with her teeth, some of her skin got caught in her braces. Daddy carried a gun but he couldn't shoot his little girl. He dropped to his knees and sobbed as Taylor pounced on him, pressing her thumbs into his eyes until she felt them burst like smashed grapes. She bent down and sucked up the mush from his eye sockets.

Her little sister escaped through the open front door, but Taylor caught her. "Where you going, little girl?" she screamed. She put her foot on her sister's chest for leverage as she tore her arm off. "Where you going?"

Once the blood stopped squirting from Libby's shoulder where her arm used to be, Taylor stood. Down the street the Biver's lights were on.

Kill everyone, Taylor thought, taking Libby's arm with her. *Killthemkillthem.*

16 Dom

Dom lived in a quiet neighborhood. There were many elderly couples in the senior citizen complex next to their apartment building. Across the road was a strip mall with a pawn shop, a Rite Aid, and some beauty parlors. Living on the outskirts of Seattle meant a somewhat less crowded population, more space, and dinky little shops no one cared about.

The perfect place to swarm for resources.

He wondered if there hadn't been a sporting goods store there, would the neighborhood have fallen into chaos as fast as it did? The lure of survival goods and ammunition was probably overwhelming to the frantic urges of desperate people. With its huge parking lot, it was easy access. If Dom lived in Seattle proper, he'd travel far to try places like this, too.

Then again, he did when he went across the bridge to Wal-Mart. And it resulted in two near death experiences.

Brian had been keeping an eye on the street after they saw a news report on a roaming gang of looters in the area when two men parked their trucks and headed for the store. They both had a handful of friends with them, but it was obvious they didn't know each other.

When the groups spotted each other, they approached the doors to the shop with hesitation. They gestured to one another. Hands up in front of them in the universal gesture for peace.

At first it seemed okay. They tugged at the doors—locked, since the store didn't open until mid-morning—then seemed to discuss something for a while. One must've said something the other didn't like, and that's when the first punch was thrown and the two groups merged into a brawl.

After the first punch landed, it went downhill from there. One pulled a gun on the other, shot and killed him, and then everyone gave up on talking or being rational. No one could ever be the hero, not when the whole city was turning against each other. Eventually someone broke the big display windows in the shop and they started scrambling in like ants.

From there, people driving by stopped and entered the fray. Some of them headed straight for the shop. Others entered the fight; whether to try and stop it or take a side, Dom wasn't sure.

Dom couldn't look once the rioting started. Brian updated him every ten minutes on what was happening. There was something about the ragtag group of neighbors fighting each other that made his gut tighten and his head spin. Soccer moms, people still in work clothes, and even a few that were definitely too young to be there.

"They finally broke the doors," Brian interjected, breaking him from his thoughts. "But they're still using the windows."

The fight spread to the Rite Aid. They were looting the stores and fleeing back to their apartments or vehicles. Despite Dom telling her she shouldn't, Chelsea joined Brian in watching from their fourth story view.

It was like a videogame. They were so displaced from it, it started to become surreal. This wasn't reality. They weren't across the street from people hammering each other's faces into the concrete, shooting each other. They weren't waiting to see who lived or who died.

And it most definitely wasn't the end of the world.

***

Dom couldn't remember what town the incident happened in. He couldn't remember what news channel he watched it on, what he'd been watching before, or what happened after. All he could remember was the sight of the naked bodies hanging from the overpass in Montana.

The camera panned across the bodies one by one, each of them mutilated with holes and gashes in their bodies, rope tied around their necks. When he saw the two children side by side, intestines looping out of their small stomachs, he heard Chelsea turn, dash into the kitchen, and retch into the sink.

"It's...it's hard to watch," the news anchor choked as the footage ended and was back on him. His face was white, eyes flat. "Reports of violent, insane acts are showing up all over areas that have been infected. Officials have reported that in some cases, infected individuals are exhibiting signs of complete insanity. These individuals cannot be reasoned with. They can be highly manipulative. We have Erik Eskilson from the CDC with more details."

It cut to a gruff man standing against a gray background. A CDC badge hung against his chest. "The rate of infection is progressing rapidly. Though the CDC does not have all the answers, please rest assured we are working nonstop to figure this thing out. What we originally thought was some type of infection similar to rabies, is actually a parasitic infection that is transmissible through even the slightest contact with infected bodily fluids. The parasite is a type of worm that utilizes the host body to replicate and mature. In its smallest form it is microscopic. They can grow up to two feet long at the biggest."

The shot cut to photographs of white, slimy creatures with rulers next to them for reference. Dom felt confusion sweep over him. Why were they just now revealing that it was a parasite? From what he knew about parasitic worms, they made you sick and could eventually kill you after they took over in your intestines. That had *nothing* to do with the bodies hanging from the overpass.

"When a healthy person comes in contact with the parasite, they fall into a coma. This is the incubation period the parasite needs in order to try and take over the host body. From this point the public is aware of the symptoms such as the yellow, foul sweat. If the host isn't capable of bearing the worm to full maturity—the big ones you just saw—they release chemicals that cause imbalances in the brain resulting in unusually cruel and violent behavior. But please remember, *they are still carriers* of the parasite. Some of them can almost pass for healthy, but *they are not*. The hosts who do bear the parasite to full maturity will rise and attempt to find a densely populated area of unaffected people before..."

The man looked at his feet, then up at the ceiling as he took a deep breath. "Listen, there's no other way to put it. They find any way they can to burst their chest cavity and stomach, releasing the parasite into the world. The parasite is relatively fast moving and can burrow through skin in moments. The only way to stop this is to stay away from any form of the parasite. Stay in your homes, stay out of the streets, and do not attempt to rescue anyone who may be a host."

The channel cut to another official who rattled off new procedures, but Dom was already holding Chelsea in his arms and didn't listen to a word he said.

This was unreal. This was worse than fucking *zombies*. You knew a zombie when you saw one. But crazy people? People with worms in their bodies waiting to *explode* on you?

75

Brian came from his room, a look on his face saying he'd learned of the news, too. "Do you think they're still hiding anything from us?"

He collapsed on the couch next to them. Chelsea had gone silent.

"I hope not. I don't see how this could get any worse."

17 Gary

When Gary LoPiccolo woke up, everything was different. The door to his room was unlocked and outside other patients wandered the hall aimlessly. There were no orderlies to be seen. He felt hot and a little agitated, like how he did when he didn't take his meds, but at least ten times worse.

And he liked it. It wasn't a bad feeling. It was one he knew well and was the reason why he was in the Greenwood Mental Facility. In the past, when that hot, tingly sensation became uncontrollable, Gary would find pretty girls to admire. To keep for himself. He'd done it many times before getting caught. What did him in was when he tried keeping more than one girl locked away in the basement of his house. They conspired and one got free.

When they caught him, they said regular prison wasn't the place for him. They said his brain was broken. Gary disagreed; he knew what he was doing. But his mother mentioned something about pleading insanity, and…Well, Gary didn't like to think about it.

Whatever nonsense they said seemed a blurry memory compared to his senses now. He had his hot and tingly sensation, but with a deeper sense of urgency. To do something. Really do *something*.

But what?

Gary peeled himself from the sweat-soaked bed and stood in his room. His arms had pus-filled wounds on them. He touched one, feeling it sting. Something wiggled under his touch, but when he moved his finger away there was nothing but a tiny stream of fresh blood.

Down the hall he heard someone crying. He followed the noise, checking for orderlies as he went. People he recognized from the rec room were out of their rooms. Oliver, an older man Gary knew, was on his butt on the floor, reaching into a pool of blood on the ground and painting the walls with it. The blood's source was under the door in front of him, still fresh and seeping. Oliver kidnapped 15 boys in his lifetime. Or at least that was what everyone said he did. Whether he did or didn't, Oliver couldn't speak to say otherwise. He had cut his own tongue out to feed to two of the boys.

That's what Oliver did; he kidnapped them and cut parts of himself off for them to eat. It's why his body was so lumpy and misshapen, from the muscle he'd been filleting off.

It became obvious the patients had mutinied. Is that what you called it? No one in charge was anywhere to be found, and the patients were either screaming or fighting each other. There was something wrong with their eyes and a truly rancid scent permeated the halls.

"Hail, LoPiccolo!"

He turned on his heel, pressing his back against the wall for defense. Coming from an Orderly Only room was Madison Cole, with loops of intestines hanging heavy on her neck.

"We got a fieldtrip bus outside ready to go."

"Go? Go where?"

Madison giggled, stroking the slick intestines. A puncture in one of them was forcing foul, lumpy juices out of it. They dribbled on her clothes. Gary didn't know what she was in for. He didn't like talking to the girls in Greenwood.

"Anywhere. We just gonna get in and drive drive drive together! No one can stop us. Can't you see, bud? We're FREE!"

She spun in a circle. Her morbid necklaces flapped against her body, eventually sliding to the floor.

"Who else is going?" Gary was cautious, especially with these crazy people.

"Um, everyone," she said as she put her intestines back over her neck. "Everyone from my hall. 'Bout half of yours. So what do you say? We're leaving right now. I just stopped to get goodies!"

Madison reached into a plastic bag, pulling out a blood smeared can of pop and a torn candy bar. Gary was accustomed to her stupidity. She didn't have an ounce of smarts in her entire body. She was dangerous and wild, like an animal, but she was offering a way out and Gary couldn't say no to that.

"Ok. I'll go with you."

"Good." Her red eyes bore into his. "The more the merrier."

18 Adam

The sweat was a defense mechanism.

Through shatterproof glass, Adam observed the husband and wife brought in from North Dakota. It was confirmed they were infected by the version of the parasite that burst through the little girl's chest cavity.

Their daughter becoming infected through blood contact. Her eventual death. Both claimed worms burrowed into them through their skin and that's how they were infected. The first sweep over their bodies did show puckered, oozing wounds in a circular pattern on their torsos.

They'd been trying to contact emergency services for their daughter but weren't able to make contact with anyone. Lindsey was unaware of the infection, but Sam had heard about the hospital massacre on the radio on the way home from work. He called the infection hotline the CDC set up and informed them of what happened.

Local CDC reps covering the breakout in the hospital descended upon their house within the hour, then transporting them to Georgia, interviewing en route. Both were shaken from the incident, but tried to explain all the circumstances to the best of their ability. The worms were big and fast, crawling up their pant legs and latching onto them. Lindsey described ripping the worms from her skin being more painful than when they first bit her. They were asked if they would be willing to undergo tests once in Georgia, to which they agreed with no hesitation.

After a couple of hours their symptoms worsened. The sweating became worse and they fell unconscious. By the time they arrived in Georgia, they'd been in comas for hours.

Even though his team couldn't run tests on them while they were conscious, Adam considered what they told them a wealth of knowledge. Not to mention their bravery and rationality in contacting the CDC, which was admirable. They were the only living infected beings they had to study. He felt terrible about their being infected—it could only mean they'd end up dead or crazy—but at least they'd be able to monitor live hosts and learn something.

His bosses enacted the obligatory "can we save them or hospitalize them" spiel, but the safety of the nation was at stake. Their fates were inevitable and Adam and his team needed to be there to see it happen. In the end, it didn't take much convincing. Besides, they had volunteered their bodies to science. All Adam had to do was drop a statistic to get them moving; North Dakota had an estimated infection rate of 67%. Drastic measures had to be taken to find a solution.

His bosses were concerned they were going to conduct inhumane experiments on the couple. *Experiment* was too dramatic of a word. Adam assured everyone they were simply going to observe and take samples. They needed to be observed through all stages—their vitals and samples taken on the hour.

"There is no way to save them," Adam assured the higher-ups. "The best thing we can do for them is use their deaths to save other people."

When Adam first went to see them after they were secured, the smell was unpleasant but not intolerable. It was sour with undertones of rotten vegetables, but he breathed through his nose and managed. As the hours progressed he didn't get used to the smell because it worsened. Beyond it being bad it actually made him feel dizzy and nauseated. If he hadn't left the room when he had, he surely would've vomited.

He realized the smell in their yellow sweat was a defense mechanism once he compared it with their decreasing vitals. Their pulses were slowing, and their incoherent mumbling ceased. The male's stomach became distended and movement, the parasite no doubt, was visible under the skin.

The chemicals in the sweat were so unbearable that it warded potential threats to the host body. Indeed, they were easy targets in their comas. It was simple and effective, much like how a skunk operated. Based on the scene photos and bodies, the young daughter exhibited the same symptom. Her bed had been saturated with sweat. Had the parents intended to take her to the hospital? Were they unable to be in her presence long enough to even move her?

He refocused his attention to the couple. Lately he'd been spending more time than anyone else inside the viewing room, simply watching the couple and scribbling notes. He could only draw himself away if he knew something *had* to be done elsewhere. The white bed sheets around them were yellowed. He watched as viscous liquid dripped from their pores. Their fevers were beyond what the human body could handle without damage to the brain.

The parasite had to protect the host body during this defenseless period. Adam wondered what would happen if they killed one of the host bodies during the gestation period. Would the worms flee the body and seek a new host? Would they eventually die inside the body? Regardless, he wanted to see these two hosts through to the end. The entire lab was abuzz, fixating on even the slightest change in vitals. Lab techs were always removed from these situations, emotionally and physically. Things came to them, they ran tests and analyzed. Adam wondered if he'd act the same way if he was in their position.

Adam imagined the parasite growing bigger inside them, using up their organs, tissue, and blood. He waited for the moment when they'd be ready to burst. He'd be prepared.

Beside him, the door beeped and swung open. It was Marla. She wasn't surprised to see him. In fact, she walked straight to him.

He glanced at his watch. "What are you doing here? Physical checks aren't for another hour. But based on your lack of hazmat suit, I don't think that's why you're here."

She pulled a chair next to him. Metal squeaked against the floor. "I'm on my way home, which, by the way, you should consider doing some time."

Adam knew the techs made up silly rumors about his "obsession" with Anisakis Nova. He overheard a guy named Kaiser in the cafeteria mention it.

"Perhaps if everyone had the same sense of devotion I do, we'd be coming up with solutions faster." The remark came off harsher than he intended, but Adam was irritated with her flippancy. "Again, what are you doing here?"

"I just had a thought, something positive that helped...I don't know, reassure me?"

Marla ran a hand through her hair. It was dark and curly, cut just above the shoulders. Very different than Gina's painstakingly styled, fake red hair. He looked away, feeling his cheeks redden slightly. He wasn't supposed to notice Marla's hair, especially considering the circumstances.

"What is it?"

"I was thinking of Ebola. It's a terrifying, powerful virus. It would be perfect, potentially even unstoppable and more destructive if it didn't kill its host so quickly."

Adam's brows rose. "Ok? What is your point?"

"The parasite we're dealing with is indeed horrible, but like Ebola it isn't perfect. From what we understand, many of the hosts exhibiting violence kill the uninfected. They don't seek to spread the parasite. Could you imagine what kind of trouble we'd be in if they consciously sought to infect other people?"

"I suppose you're right. However, I think it makes up for that one flaw in many other ways."

Marla continued as though she didn't hear him. "And look at those two! The hosts are in a coma for an extended period of time. If we started seeking out and killing host bodies rather than trying to detain or save them, imagine what a dent we could put in stopping this thing."

"It is a rapidly mutating genus of nematode we've never heard of. For all you know, within a month it will have evolved beyond such a long coma stasis," Adam said, intent on getting his point through. "Not to mention, if the parasite learned to secrete less chemicals that cause said violent behavior, the host *could* develop more intelligent behavior."

She frowned. "Don't think that, Dr. Baker."

"Why? Because thinking it will make it true?" Adam laughed, but it was bitter. "Positive thinking and 'what-ifs' aren't going to get us anywhere."

Marla stood quickly, closing the distance between her and the door. Before she left she looked back. "The second you start losing hope, we don't really have a reason to keep trying."

Adam was left with his own thoughts, only now they weren't so focused.

***

On the fourth day, as he would've expected, Lindsey Price woke from her coma. At first she laid there, red eyes scanning the room back and forth. It seemed she was trying to figure out where she was. Two lab techs came in to take samples. They got so far as doing the usual sweat tests when she became violent and wanted to kill.

Then she thrashed wildly in her bed. Had she not been tied down she would've done damage to herself and the room. The lab techs ran out and retrieved security. Guards in hazmat suits came in and tried to sedate her. It did nothing. Eventually she got one hand free from the restraints.

"I'm going to kill you," she said in a loud, yet disturbingly flat tone. She repeated it until the words blurred together. It took a moment before Adam realized she was saying it to her unconscious husband.

"Gonna shove a bottle of vodka down your throat," she said calmly. "Gonna make you drown on it."

Eventually she lost interest in Sam Price and focused on the guards. Her nails broke against their plastic face guards as she clawed. One guard panicked and shot her in the head.

At a glance her stomach wasn't as bloated, her symptoms overall lesser than the husband. When they carted her body away for an autopsy, they discovered parasites only a centimeter in length; that was a fraction of the smallest they found from the daughter's body. They hadn't matured for whatever reason. Incompatible genetics, Marla said. The parasites were alive and her body was moved to a separate cell where scientists would study how long the parasites could live in a dead host. The two techs had just enough time to see her sweating had stopped; all that was left on her skin was old and dried. It meant that, technically, they wouldn't smell if they washed the residue off.

But on that fourth day, when the male host should've woken up or exploded, or *something*, like the female, he did nothing. He was still alive and his stomach showed signs of parasitic activity, but the big bang hadn't happened yet.

What was he missing? What made the first generations of hosts go insane, but not manifest the parasites in their fullest form? It wasn't a generalized step in their evolution. The spread of infection had crossed into North Dakota's bordering states, and while some reports of the parasite had occurred, most were still exhibiting merely violent behavior.

He shuddered. The lack of predictability or logic scared him. Things he was positive about before were being challenged on almost an hourly basis.

His lunch had grown cold. He stared at the cheese steak sandwich and imagined a microscopic parasite lurking within. The thought of a multitude of parasitic specimens in a lab nearby did nothing to soothe his nerves.

Gina was even more worried. Their twenty-two years of marriage hadn't been easy and with everything going on, it was made worse. Adam had only been home twice since the start of the infection, and it was only to get a change of clothes.

The second he stepped through the door Gina was on him. They fought. Gina wanted to drive three hours north to pick up their daughters from the university and stay home. He said no; they were tough and would be okay. His true reasoning was selfish; first, he had high hopes the infection wouldn't reach them. Second, he simply didn't have the time to leave his work to pick them up. He hadn't felt more useful or like himself until recently. Coming back home, even if he did care about his daughters, created a sense of dread for him.

In a desperate attempt to reassure her and end the argument, he said they took after her in that they were strong and persevered. Feeding into Gina's vanity usually helped end their fights.

That had been a bad move, apparently, because Gina started screaming about how he never cared about her or their daughters. Adam couldn't—*wouldn't*—take the abuse. He packed his suitcase with anything he thought he'd need for the next few weeks and left without another word to his wife. In the grand scheme of things, his fight with her meant nothing. Adam wished she would understand that.

Later that day Helen and Madeline each texted him individually, saying they were on a Greyhound home after a hysterical call from mom. It wasn't a courtesy notification, or that they wanted to know if he was okay. Instead they wondered when he'd be home so they could use his car. The request wounded Adam, but he knew they were always on Gina's side. This shouldn't have surprised him.

Now he sat at his desk, reviewing what happened with the female host and everything they had up to date. In front of him the Word document was blank, save for the standard header and footer. The cursor blinked. This far into the infection, he'd hoped he would have more to say. More results and contingency plans.

With no real ideas in his mind, he began typing, hoping something would come to him. Perhaps if he used enough big words and terms, his bosses wouldn't bother reading that he had no concrete news to report.

19 Dr. Marla Ainsworth

Lindsey Price was dead. Marla was devastated by the loss, not only because Lindsey was a person, but because Marla developed an irrational idea that she could save her before she woke up from her coma.

There was that, at least. Her advancements in planning a framework to synthesize a cure. She was sure she was close to something. Her ideas were solid, but it was the execution and logistics that were holding her down. Even though she disliked Chandler, she was going to ask him and Suresh to assist her. She simply couldn't do all the work on her own.

Everyone's workdays were long, some people sleeping in their offices or the break room. The stale scent of unwashed bodies, coffee, and energy drinks was becoming noticeable. Marla liked to work herself hard just like everyone else, but there came a point when your brain was ineffective and needed to recharge. Today was one of those days.

She was taking a half day at home before she planned on returning to the lab to get down and dirty and start synthesizing. As usual, the second she walked in and was embraced by the familiar scent of her lavender potpourri and even the smell of Doom, she felt better. With a takeout order of enchiladas, chips, and plenty of salsa and guacamole before her, she ran down the idea for the cure again.

A variety of antihelminthics were used on the infected the moment the CDC discovered it was a parasite. They were simple enough; administered orally, they would cause a chemical reaction in the parasite that would kill the larvae. Some antihelminthics were ovicidal, killing the egg. None of the existing antihelminthics proved effective. People had given up quickly because it was presumed *Anisakis* larvae couldn't survive inside the human body, rendering the drugs useless. But this was *Anisakis Nova,* as Dr. Baker called it. This was different.

Marla looked at it this way: the worms were resistant to known antihelminthics. It was obvious an alternate drug must be created to combat it.

That was exactly what Marla intended to do.

She believed she could synthesize a chemical that would stop infection. All antihelminthics were similar; they stopped the parasite from developing from egg into adult form by blocking their ability to digest nutrients.

But she had her work cut out for her. She needed to know what *exactly* was stopping the current drugs from working and how to trick the parasite into absorbing it. She needed ample test subjects in stage 1 to test the drug on, assuming she could create it. The worms grew so large, so quickly, she knew the only chance they had of killing them in body was in the stopping them from fully maturing. She needed to create a resilient, superior version that would kill them in egg stage, or at the very least stop them from growing.

When Marla started thinking about it all, a moment of panic rang through her entire body. It was all possible if she had enough time. Research like this took months, more likely years. It required identifying the exact mutation of Anisakis to Anisakis Nova, then figuring out how to counter that specific change.

But time was what everyone was in short supply of. The infection was spiraling out from North Dakota at an exponential rate. It would be in Georgia before the week was out if authorities weren't able to contain it. She knew the government had stockpiles of antivirals that would only be used under pandemic circumstances. But that was for influenza, not a parasite. Yet the principal would most likely be the same; if she came up with something that she believed *could* work, the desperate need for it would bypass most testing and it would be administered immediately to prevent further devastation on the country.

They'd literally be brewing up something in the lab and sending it out.

The food started to taste flat as guilt cropped up. Here she was, relaxing and eating, when she could be at the lab. It was conflicting; she knew she needed to rest but she didn't want to.

Marla put the leftovers in the fridge and locked Doom in the bathroom with his litter box and food. She needed as much uninterrupted sleep as she could manage before going back.

20 The Infected

Diane wasn't going to take her kids to the quarantine zone no matter what any news anchor or government official told her. Her sister's cousin told her they were killing infected people at the quarantine zones. Then her brother's second wife told her the only thing to do was to outrun the infection to the coast.

She had to move fast if she was going to meet up with Sean's family. Spokane was a hell of a drive away from the coast of Washington, but it was her kids and she'd do anything to keep them. Ever since Sean left the picture she was much happier.

No daddy and two girls? Plus the fact that she got an injury "on the job" a few years back? The welfare checks were fat and did her just fine, especially when she managed to sell a little weed on the side. The kids were her ticket to the good life—she'd have another if she could—and no one was taking them away.

But what she'd seen at the bus depot was enough to make anyone afraid to go it alone. Sean was the muscle in the relationship. If anyone ever looked at Diane wrong it was Sean who beat the hell out of them. She was happier without him, but she'd kill to have him watching her back since all this virus stuff started happening.

The sick people were everywhere. They were ripping people apart like they were nothing. There was so much blood and so much screaming, it was a wonder she made it out alive.

After the scene at the depot, Diane knew she had to get a car and get herself out of there. On her own. She put Brandy and Miley in a safe spot by some Goodwill donation bins and stalked a Rite Aid parking lot for someone weak. Eventually an older lady showed up by herself. Diane pulled a knife on her, the very one she'd stolen from Sean, and hijacked her car.

Diane dragged the girls to the car. She almost had to carry Brandy, who stumbled like she was drunk. She'd kept saying she was sick. The second Diane got her into the car she fell asleep and stayed that way as they crossed the mountains. Diane wasn't sure if it was that Miley, the baby, needed to be changed or something died in the radiator, because there was a righteous stench in the car that was making her sick, too.

It had been seven hours driving. They got rerouted five times because of traffic revisions. Diane needed to take a break. Her body was stiff and Miley had been crying for an hour straight. For a two year old she sure was dependent. Diane would leave Brandy alone for an entire day at a time when she was four, and nothing bad ever happened. Taught her to be independent. Like her mama always told her, you can't take care of yourself, you can't take care of no one.

She pulled over on a truck runaway ramp and got out of the car. The fresh air felt good. Then she realized how quiet it was.

Miley stopped crying.

She went to the backdoor and peered through the window. Brandy was awake, staring straight ahead through the windshield. Miley...

Miley wasn't moving.

Diane tried opening the door but it was locked. She tried the driver's door, but it was locked, too. The keys were inside.

"Brandy," she screamed. "You let me in right now!"

Diane tried the other doors twice. Her daughter didn't flinch as she beat her fists against the window, screaming for her to let her in. After ten minutes, Diane gave up. She sat on the gravel and took out a cigarette, wishing she had something better to soothe her nerves.

"Can't take care of yourself, mama?"

Diane yelped, stumbling to her feet and spinning around. Behind her stood Brandy. But something was off. Her eyes were bloodshot and it looked like she'd puked on herself. But that wasn't going to save her from the beating Diane was about to deliver.

"You little shit, what were you doing in there?"

"Can't take care of yourssssself, mama? Mama?" Her voice sounded broken. Like she was having to think hard for every word, forgetting them as she spoke.

Despite the fear welling inside her, and her instincts telling her not to, Diane stepped up to Brandy and raised her hand to slap her.

Then she saw the flash of a blade just as Brandy rammed it into her lower abdomen. She dropped to her knees, the blade sliding out of her body as she went, pressing her hands against herself to stop the flow of blood.

"No more babies for you, mama." Brandy dropped to her knees, bringing the knife over her head. She brought it down, plunging it into Diane's stomach. "No more babies. No babies."

Diane's blood splattered her daughter's face. The world was starting to fade.

"Hate you," Brandy screamed with each drop of the knife. "Hate you."

21 Dom

The day the first incident of infection popped up in Seattle was the beginning of the end. Before that, Dom's hope the parasite wouldn't reach Washington never wavered. Part of him thought the government would take care of it eventually, that it was only a matter of time before it was under control. When he watched the news, he felt anxious and angry, but it was just the same as when he saw footage of war or natural disasters. Yes, it was tragic. But at the end of the day it didn't affect him. It wasn't a few blocks away threatening his life and the lives of his loved ones.

Now it did. Now it was going to affect all of them.

A bus driven by one of the crazy infected barreled off the highway and rammed through a grocery store. It was packed with more infected, from a mental institution no less, armed to the teeth with wicked makeshift weapons. After slaughtering everyone in the store they dispersed into the city, leaving droves of wounded and potentially infected people in their wake.

Martial law was enacted within hours of the event. There was a 24 hour curfew; anyone on the streets would be detained or dispatched. Dom knew what that meant for most people who weren't lucky enough to have food storage or supplies.

"It won't work," Brian insisted as they wolfed down their rations of Chef Boyardee. "People might stay inside for a day at most, but then they'll get antsy. Or hungry. Or something will drive them out, but once they're all out it will be even worse than it is now."

Dom and Chelsea were silent. His food tasted too metallic and congealed, its color too red. Brian was right about one thing. Since the curfew had been enacted, people quieted down. The fighting in the strip mall dwindled to nothing. The neighborhood was holding its breath, waiting for something to happen.

But what?

"We need to decide what the plan is," Chelsea said.

"Meaning?" Brian was rearing for a fight. Dom noticed the more scared his friend was, the more he tried provoking Chelsea.

"Well, are we going to try and wait things out here or make a run for the country?"

"God, Chelsea! This isn't a movie! If we leave we're going to get shot!" Brian pointed his fork at her. "You're so fucking stupid. 'Make a run for the country.' You're acting like we have some glorious place to go to."

"Stop it. Both of you." Dom was impressed by the strength of his own voice. They both shut up, but the tension was heavy in the air. "Brian, you're right. Chelsea, you're also right. If we go out there we risk getting killed by infected people, the police, *and* anyone else. But if we stay here, we risk being surrounded by thousands of potentially infected people. There's nothing between us and the world except our front door."

Brian poked at the remaining scraps of his ravioli. "Like I was saying, we don't have a plan for leaving the apartment. I'm not sure where we'd go if we left. We don't know anyone who has a cabin or anything. We don't have the right gear to backpack into the wilderness or the know-how."

He was trying to be helpful, so Dom gave him an encouraging smile and nod. "Good point. We'd have to drive for miles on the freeway before even hitting places not so densely populated. I guess the question is, what do we do to make it safe here? Chelsea, any thoughts?"

"Find out who is still here. Are you on friendly terms with anyone? Maybe we should invite Sadie and her kid in here. Pool resources and start forming a group. We could block the front door somehow?" Chelsea stared at her food, then added, "But we have to have a way to get out still. If our plan is to stay here, we at least need to come up with an escape plan. Especially with what's going on outside."

"I don't agree with grouping up with people. What if they don't have food or water? Then they're just using ours and reducing our chances of surviving," Brian said.

As much as Dom loved Chelsea, he had to agree with Brian. Chelsea had a big heart, but it was definitely going to get her killed if she wasn't careful. "I think we should shove some furniture in the front entrance downstairs. We don't have the tools to board it up, but maybe if we push the lobby furniture in front of it that will help."

"What about everyone else?"

Brian huffed and stood, taking his dish to the sink. "Screw everyone else. They should be glad we're taking action."

Dom leaned over, placing his hand on the small of her back. "I know you want to help, but I think it's better if we don't advertise how much we have. We can find out who is still here and who needs help, then go from there. Okay?"

Chelsea nodded. "I guess. You're the one who calls the shots, right? Unofficial leader of whatever this is."

"Don't be like that, Chels. I'm only trying to be a middle ground for all of us."

Another nod, but she was shutting down. She did that a lot. Dom knew all girls did. When they got pissed they were quiet, the only words uttered from their lips, 'Fine' or 'Okay.' He knew he wasn't the bad guy, but she sure as hell made him feel like it.

"Let's handle the door first while things are quiet outside," Dom said. "On the way up we'll scout out whoever is left. I have a feeling there aren't that many. Most people seemed to try and jump ship a few days ago."

"Is this the point where one of us plays bitch and has to stay behind to guard the stuff?"

"It won't be me," Chelsea spat at Brian.

"For the last time; you two need to quit it the fuck out. Understood?"

Brian joined Chelsea in her quiet mood for the rest of the day. Dom was quickly growing tired of being the only emotionally stable person in the group, and the only one willing to negotiate. He was doing the best he could. At least they followed his commands, which made their tasks a little easier.

The double doors into the small apartment building were easy to barricade. The lobby area had a battered couch and coffee table they laid vertically against the doors. It was heavy, taking all of their combined strength to get it into place. Once they were done, Dom felt safer.

He hadn't been on the first level in days. Looking out at street level was unsettling. There were blood smears on the ground and litter everywhere. A few mangled cars blocked the road to their right. Dom risked staying at the window a little longer to peer down the left for Brian's car. He told him to pay extra to use the closed off parking lot on the side of the building, but he refused. He was going to regret it.

The windshield had a mess of cracks radiating from multiple impact areas. The tires appeared to be flat. Even if they wanted to go somewhere, they didn't have a ride to do it.

Chelsea was peering through the window on the other side of the door. "I think I see someone in the salon."

Dom turned his focus to the salon in the strip mall. A man and woman were walking into it. He walked a little strangely, but other than that the couple appeared normal. Dom figured they were seeking shelter in the salon because of the curfew.

"Let's close the blinds and get out of here." Dom dropped the blinds on his window and went to Chelsea. "Don't want people to see us if we can avoid it."

They searched the first three floors for people and discovered only three families remained. Sadie and her kid and two Mexican families that spoke barely a few words of English. They were nice, but only long enough to open the door and say they didn't need help. Sadie appeared to be in good shape. She was glad Brett never came back and, although her son was afraid, they didn't have TV or internet so they hadn't seen the atrocities. She was keeping up to date through a phone call a day with her mother. And keeping track of what was going on outside.

He was envious. If Sadie had constant access to the news like they did and saw all the horrific, terrible things, she wouldn't be so upbeat.

Dom hesitantly asked if she needed anything, only because it would be hell to pay from Chelsea if he didn't. She said no and thanked them. Dom felt Brian's sigh of relief. He was relieved, too.

22 Sadie

Sadie was good at keeping a happy face even when everything in her life was at its worst. As Dom asked if she was okay, she told them just enough of the truth to make the lies easier to say. The truth was, she *did* know what was going on. She had a smart phone—God, she did have a smartphone! What did they take her for?—and read all the updates and watched all the gruesome videos. She knew exactly what was going on.

And the real truth was, if Dom wanted to enter the apartment under any circumstances, and neared Jon's room, they would've smelled it. They would've known an infected was in the building.

Sadie paid an extra hundred dollars a month to have one of the apartments that had a small patio. She had a green thumb and loved to grow things, so she'd maximized the space for a tiny year-round garden.

Jon loved to play outside. They had a bird bath and he liked to play with his action figures in it. He didn't understand why she said it was off limits, and while Sadie was making lunch he slipped out to play.

She heard him scream and when she came out, saw him holding onto a thin worm trying to burrow its way into his calf. It was impossible to grip. Her nails dug into it, blood and pus seeping out from the crescent shape they left.

It only took seconds to pull it out and toss it over the balcony. She carried Jon in, pouring rubbing alcohol into the wound despite his ear-piercing screams. His crying died down as she bandaged it with a *Tranformers* themed bandage and she rocked him in her arms.

Her own tears flowed down her cheeks. This meant her son was infected. The worm hadn't gotten in, but wasn't that all it took? Just a bit of contact? She put Jon in his bed, bringing the mini DVD-player in so he could watch a movie. Eventually he fell asleep, his breath deep.

Then the sickness. The coma. The sweat.

Jon was her only child. The only good thing in her life, even if it came from a bad decision with a bad man. Whatever happened to him, she would be there.

She would be his mom.

23 Gary

Gary LoPiccolo wanted to add the pretty girl from the apartment to his flock of hens. She would fit right in with the other ladies. Gary kept a tidy coop in the salon across from the apartment. He figured she'd be very happy there once she got to know the other girls.

He stroked the shotgun he'd taken from the dead man outside. It was a good find. It kept the ladies in line when they tried to fly away. Although he wasn't quite sure how many bullets were in it—do shotguns have bullets?— whenever he waved it at them they shrieked then quieted down.

There was Ashley, Susan, Angela, Tiffany, and Heather. He hadn't named one of the girls yet, but she looked sort of like a boy so he thought Jordan might be fitting. He found her trying to scavenge supplied in the sports store next door all by herself. A girl is no good without a flock or a man to keep them, so he got her to come next door.

Gary was good at playing nice, just until he got what he wanted. He knew getting on the bus at Greenwood was risky. Everyone on the bus was crazy before the wormies got them. They talked to themselves. Sometimes they even hurt themselves. They did bad things. The worms made them even worse, so much that they made bad decisions that got them caught.

But not Gary. He felt a little odd since he got sick, but really he had a great sense of clarity about what he wanted and how to get it.

He knew he had to wear glasses so they couldn't see his eyes, which were a little gross, he had to admit. He washed the ooze that dripped from his mouth and made sure his clothes looked nice. It took a lot to stop the involuntary jerking of his limbs, but the girls were so afraid they didn't notice.

Madison saw a grocery store and started shrieking about needing a pregnancy test and ran the entire bus right into it. After the dust settled and he reoriented, Gary couldn't stop himself from wasting time killing and raping everyone in sight like the others. Once he got a hold of himself and remembered he had a plan, he quietly slipped away and walked until he found a nice little place to build up his coop.

Being free, it seemed the logical thing to do was to finish the work he'd started before he got caught. Gary didn't know all the details, but the world was changing. There were many people like him and they were doing whatever they wanted. No one would catch Gary. Not when there were more important things going on.

It didn't take long before he gathered the six ladies. It was when he was leading Jordan into the coop that he spotted the girl in the apartment building.

She was looking outside right towards him—with a look of longing, perhaps?—when a man pulled her aside and they were gone. Gary studied them for another day and pinpointed their location to be in an apartment on the fourth floor.

He had to have her. She was pretty. She was obviously captive, abducted by those wimpy boys she was with. She wanted to escape that building and join him.

Susan was silent. Normally she was always weeping. She was on her side facing the wall, her wrists swollen and raw where they were tied to a chair bolted in the ground. Susan had been so pretty when he first found her only a few hours earlier, but she was very fragile. Gary had a special place in his heart for Susan, so he loved her more than the other girls. Her body felt good in his hands. He felt good inside of her. He'd loved her many times since he found her the previous day. Maybe he did it too much?

He poked her with the gun. "Susan, wake up." Again, harder this time. The other girls whimpered. "I said wake up. I said wake up *now*."

Then Gary smelled something. Something sweet. Familiar. He flipped her body over and noticed her shallow breathing. The yellow sweat beginning to trickle down her forehead.

He stroked her forehead, a grin on his face.

24 Adam

In the middle of the night the male host woke from his coma. It wasn't because he was dead, or that he'd exploded. It was because he wanted to talk.

Adam had been in the observing room all night. The three guards on duty were uncomfortable with his presence. It was probably because he never spoke to them; his eyes stayed glued on the figure as he scribbled notes wildly at the slightest shift in the host's vitals. It wasn't as though he didn't like the men—they both seemed fine—it was that Adam couldn't spare an iota of energy towards anything not relating to the parasite. If that meant he was coming off as a stiff, then so be it.

When the host finally woke, Adam shot from his chair and pressed against the glass to watch. Six days. They had new live host victims in another part of the lab, but they weren't nearly as close to maturing. This was it; what he had been waiting for. Whatever caused the little girl's chest to explode was about to happen. The host's vitals were through the roof: high pulse, blood pressure, and body temperature.

The man thrashed about on the bed, pulling at the restraints. The bed rocked. The sheets slipped from his body revealing the grotesquely distended stomach. It was freakish, as though he were pregnant. The parasite writhed beneath the skin.

Then he turned and looked through the glass right at Adam. His eyes were bloody, some kind of viscous opaque substance seeping from his tear ducts. Around his mouth, saliva was crusted. His tongue lolled out of his mouth, swollen and black.

"Hi there," he whispered. "Hi, hi, hi there. Come here."

Adam gulped. He looked at the guards who remained still. Finally, he pressed the intercom button. "Mr....Mr. Price?"

"That's me. Sammy Sam Price." His voice hissed the S in his name. This is what the reports of mental instability must've meant. The way he spoke...well, it wasn't normal.

"How are you feeling?" was all Adam could think to ask. Now faced with a mature host, he wasn't sure what to do.

"Like I want to rip my fucking guts out all over you and *kill kill kill* you."

Adam's chest was tight. "Why is that?"

"Because I feel like it. Because I want to tear the balls off that guard and feed them to the dogs at home, then slit the other one's throat and—"

"Do you know what happened to your wife?" Adam intended to startle the man. It worked, though not in the way he thought it would. Sam's brow furrowed as though concentrating.

"Wife."

"She's dead. She wanted to kill you. Why would she do that?"

Sam arched his back and screamed. "Don't care! That fucking cu—"

Adam released the intercom button, not hearing the rest of the sentence.

"Dr. Baker, shouldn't we be calling someone?" one of the guards asked.

"Who are we going to call? *I* am who you call." Adam took a deep breath, his gaze still averted from the lunatic on the other side of the glass. "Just...just give me another minute, okay? We don't know how long he'll be coherent."

"Not sure if coherent is the right word," the other mumbled.

Adam held down the intercom button again. "Mr. Price, do you remember how you were infected?"

"*Infected?* I feel great, just fine and dandy."

"Do you remember what happened to your daughter?"

This time he squeezed his eyes shut. Liquid streamed down his face. He let out an agonizing howl and tried to escape again.

"Please tell me something," Adam begged. "People are dying!"

Price grinned, locking eyes with Adam again. "Good. Good. *Goody good.* Want to fucking kill them, fucking tear them apart."

Fine, if that's what you want, then blow up, Adam thought. *That's what we want to see.*

One of the host's hands broke free.

"Get in there!" Adam shouted to the guards, notions of protocol and safety escaping him. What if the man killed himself somehow? Before they could study what they needed to? "Restrain the host before he hurts himself!"

They glanced at each other. None of them had hazmat suits on. It would be breaking protocol to enter without one. Plus the patient was obviously violent and strong. Adam flew to his feet. They didn't have much time. He'd risk his own life to ensure the specimen wasn't harmed.

He moved towards the door. "If you don't go, I'll go myself!"

That got them. The last thing they needed was punishment for disobeying orders *and* letting a scientist get killed. Adam felt a surge of guilt, like a young child being reprimanded for their selfishness. He knew he was putting the guards' lives at risk, but if anything were to happen to this host...

"Hunt, go. Charles, go get backup," said one of them. Hunt clicked the safety off his gun and went into the first safety chamber. The other guard keyed in a code. One door slid open. A moment later the other opened into the lab.

The host freed his other hand. As the guard entered the room and approached, his aggression levels increased as he honed in on him. The guard approached, unsure of what to do now that the host was half-way freed. Price started shouting about balls again and everything he'd do to the guard.

Whatever decision Hunt planned on making, he ended up not having to decide.

The host laid down and arched his back, using his own hands to tear through the taut skin of his stomach, lifting his belly into the air as thousands of parasites burst from it.

A handful of them landed directly on the guard. They were fast and surprisingly agile. The ones on the ground and bed migrated towards him, flopping off the bed in a mess of bodily fluids and blood. The ones on him crawled up to his exposed face and latched on.

The guard panicked and grabbed at them. He moved towards the door, screaming for help. His hand slapped against the door release button, sending it flying open. He stumbled in, still clawing at his face.

As the other guard went to let him back in, Adam grabbed his shoulder. "You can't do that! They'll get in here."

They looked at each other and to their companion.

"Fuck you, Baker!"

He opened the door just as Hunt came barreling in, knocking the other guard to the ground and running straight into Adam. His gurgling screams were slowly fading as the worms made their way into his mouth and down his throat.

Adam fell backward as Hunt toppled onto him. Hot, slimy worms slapped against his face as Hunt desperately tried to get them off. It took every bit of strength Adam had to shove him aside and crawl away. He gripped a thin worm, about as big and thick as a pencil, peeling it off his face. A sharp pain stung on his cheek as he yanked the worm free.

Panic took hold of every fiber of Adam's being. *I'm infected, I'm infected, oh God I'm infected.* He looked to the other guard. His heel hit a parasite as he flung himself around. As he went down they overtook him, wriggling into any openings in his clothes. They crowded his face and, before long, there was nothing to be seen except a pile of white worm-like creatures with only glimpses of the body beneath them.

Adam scrambled to his feet and left the room, clutching his bleeding cheek. Were there more on him? Had they gotten into his clothes? Was a few seconds truly all the parasite needed to infect him?

He felt as though a million of them were crawling on his skin. As he ran back to his office he kept patting at his body, only to verify that he couldn't feel any.

25 The Infected

Rick Lavender wasn't looking forward to work that night. Half his buddies already said they weren't coming in to work until things blew over, or in some cases never again since they thought it was the end of the world. But Rick always had a good work ethic and he saw no real reason not go in. He'd been working night security at the Georgia CDC location for six years now and not a single day missed.

Besides, North Dakota was states away. The infection had reached Montana, but nowhere else according to the news. He was going in to work—despite his wife's protests—and that was that.

Only that night was turning out to be the worst night to come in. It started with a call from the third quadrant of the building for backup security on a possible hostile situation. That was already bad. Nothing ever went on during the night shift. As Rick trekked across the campus, he prepared to draw his gun; something he'd never done on the job. On the way he met up with another guard responding to the call. It was Chuck Fehd, someone he worked with frequently.

"Any idea what this is about?"

"No," Rick answered. "But isn't that quadrant where they're storing infected people?"

Fehd shrugged. "Beats me." He ran his security card through a door leading to a higher security area of the building.

As they rounded a corner they saw another guard slumped against a door, his body visibly shaking. The two ran over and knelt by him. He was muttering incoherently about worms, and Cole, and balls getting cut off.

Fehd shot Rick a wary look. They weren't getting anything from him, but whatever hostile situation was happening was behind the door.

Rick drew his gun and ran his card. The door swung open into a room with a giant floor to ceiling window on the left and another door straight ahead.

"Oh, God."

He wasn't sure if he said it or Fehd, but the sight behind the window was enough to make anyone want to meet their maker. On a gurney in the other room a man's body lay, his ribs burst outward from the gaping hole in his torso. Blood and flecks of gore were everywhere, splattered against the window, ground, and wall. On the floor another guard laid motionless, bloodied.

"What the *fuck* happened in there," Fehd whispered.

"I don't know but we need to help that guy. I think it's Hunt," Rick said as he went to the other door. He ran his card through. Fehd followed behind him. They had to pass through another security door before entering the room. Where was the hostile threat? Had it moved?

What am I getting myself into?

The scent of human bodily fluids and something else, something more acrid, hit Rick's nose and made him gag. He brought his sleeve to his nose as he rushed over to Hunt, bending down to check his pulse.

"He's alive."

"Well let's get him the hell out of here," Fehd said, eyeing the corpse. "What the fuck are they doing in here? The CDC studies diseases, they don't do fucking...fucking crazy experiments!"

"Calm down. Just help me drag him out of here, okay? It looks like he's bleeding."

"Lavender and Fehd, please report your location."

Rick paused to click the button on his radio. "This is Lavender. We reported to the hostile situation. We're recovering officer Hunt."

"Get out of that room, Lavender. Get out of that room right now!"

"Hey, what's that?"

Rick turned in time to see big white worms seeping from the vent above Fehd. One landed on his shoulder and slapped on the ground. But it was fast. It was crawling up Fehd before he moved an inch. The flow of worms increased until a mass of them seeped from it.

"What the f—"

Rick's body took over. He dodged beside Fehd who was now screaming as he slipped and fell, his head cracking against the window.

Rick reached for his security card when he felt something hot and slimy against his shoulder. He glanced down to see a white, shapeless worm five inches long cling to his fingers. They were on him, all over him. He felt panic, pure and primal, surge through his body as he flung himself around wildly in hopes of dislodging them.

The worms wriggled their way up his neck. He tried to beat them away, but they clung to his clothing and made his fingers sting as they brushed against him. He thought of his wife, at home waiting for him to call during his break, of the guys who decided not to come in.

He thought of his perfect attendance record, how even in death he wasn't going to ruin it.

Then he felt the first one begin fighting its way into his mouth, tiny teeth grinding away at his lips. His hearing dampened as he felt smaller worms wriggle into his ears. He thought of nothing but the searing pain in his body as the tiny ones got under his clothes, pinpricks of pain all over his torso as they burrowed into his body.

When the worm finally got into his mouth, it went straight down his throat into his stomach, shredding and eating Rick's insides as its brethren followed suit.

26 Dom

Outside, the chaos reached its crescendo. Dom and Brian huddled in the bathroom, the farthest room from the windows, as stray bullets shattered glass and thudded in the wall. Chelsea lay in the bathtub in a fetal position, her body shaking. It was obvious she was crying, but she said to leave her alone. Dom wanted nothing more than to hold her and tell her it was going to be okay. Not being able to only added to his misery.

The previous day passed in pleasant quietness. They played Monopoly and made a huge dinner since they were in such good spirits. It wasn't until midway through the night that the first gun fired and from there...well, that was it. They watched for a little while, but once the first bullet hit their building they retreated as far away from the walls as they could.

"We should have left when we had the chance," Brian groaned. "We don't stand a chance now."

"You're the one that said we shouldn't leave," Chelsea said. "You said we had nowhere to go and we couldn't make it."

Dom pressed his face into his hands. He could barely keep his eyes open but was too afraid to sleep. As much as he hated Brian's incessant whining, it was the only thing distracting him from fixating on the noise outside.

"Before we had to get *your* sorry ass I wanted to get out of here. Right, Dom?"

Dom couldn't remember. He couldn't think. It didn't matter who said what. He just wanted the gunfire and screaming to stop. "Brian, why don't you get your phone out and try to find out what is going on."

Brian opened his mouth for a rebuttal, but an explosion somewhere across town shut him up. The fighting outside subsided for a moment, as though everyone stopped to listen. Then someone fired and it started again.

"Oh, God."

Brian's jaw dropped and his head sagged. The glow of his phone illuminated his wide eyes. He handed the phone to Dom.

It was a painfully brief announcement on KOMO News from the state that they were carpet bombing the entire city within a ten mile radius. The goal was to prevent the spread of the parasite and kill as many infected as possible. There were evacuation sites where they claimed to be bussing uninfected people out to safe zones.

A map with a red circular overlay on Seattle and neighboring cities showed the bombing radius. While they were on the fringe of it, there was no doubt they'd get hit. The closest evacuation zone was the middle school a few miles south from their location. The bombings would take place in approximately 48 hours. How did they jump from martial law and curfews to leveling the entire city?

Was that why people were losing it outside? In their mad attempt to flee the city?

"How can they do this?" Dom said, his question distant and unsure.

Realizing something was wrong, Chelsea sat up. "What is it?"

He handed her the phone, unable to repeat what he'd just read. Chelsea set the phone on the edge of the tub, sinking back in behind the shower curtain, silent.

"This is a joke," Dom whispered. "Someone hacked the website. It's a sick joke."

It had to be. There was no way the government would up and bomb a city like that. Didn't they need approval? Wasn't there authorization and protocol? Dom grabbed the phone and began checking all the other local news websites to be sure. Each one showed the exact same message.

"I'm leaving."

Brian's voice was oddly level. It scared Dom. His best friend stood and walked out of the bathroom as he and Chelsea watched in disbelief.

"Get him," Chelsea cried. "He's going to get himself killed."

Dom stumbled to his feet and grabbed Brian as he b-lined it for the bug-out bags and weapons by the door.

"Brian, you can't do this. You're going to get shot out there, or infected, or God knows what!"

He jerked his shoulder away and hoisted his backpack on. "I'm leaving," he repeated. "I don't care what you do, but I'm not staying here to get bombed. I'd rather risk it out there."

"We should all go together."

"Are you fucking kidding me? This is pathetic. We thought we were hot shit with all our gear and our food, but none of it matters. Tomorrow we're going to be burnt to a crisp. Everything in here will be *gone*."

"This could be a joke," Dom said, grasping at any reason he could. "We don't know this is even real."

Brian took the assault rifle from the weapons pile. Dom's rifle. "Doesn't matter. Real or not, we've been kidding ourselves. In real life, you can't hole up in an apartment and survive the end of the world. This is the wakeup call we needed."

"Hey, you can go but you can't take my stuff," Dom snapped. He felt his face reddening. If he couldn't talk sense into Brian, he had to try something else. To distract him, at least, until he had a better idea. "You're staying here."

Brian lifted the gun, pointing it at Dom's head. "I'm leaving."

His mind blanked the second he was staring down the barrel of the rifle. He wasn't sure who the person was that stood in front of him. It wasn't his roommate anymore. It wasn't his friend since high school. It was a stranger, someone he once knew turned into a monster in a week. Like everyone else.

"Fine. Go. But the second you walk out that door, you aren't coming back in."

The front door slamming shut was his goodbye. Dom stared at the door. He checked the peephole, part of him hoping Brian still stood there. That he could convince him to stay. Despite the constant arguing, there was safety in numbers.

It took a moment, but the world finally rushed back in around him. The noises, the fear. The impending bombings that would kill them if the infected didn't do it first. Joke or not, everything was crashing around him. Dom dropped to his knees and crawled back to the bathroom where Chelsea sat in silence.

"Brian is gone. I told him not to come back."

Chelsea climbed out of the tub. Her brown hair was a mess of tangles. Her eyes were red from crying. She crawled to him and hesitantly put her arms around his neck. Dom collapsed into her grip, holding onto her. "What happened?"

"He pulled a gun on me. God, I swear I didn't recognize the person I was looking at." Dom rested his cheek against her head. "I didn't know what to do."

"You did the right thing," she said. "He was losing it. What else could you have done?"

Despite her comfort, Dom felt like it wasn't right. They had many ups and downs, but Brian was still his best friend. It was unimaginable that either of them would end the friendship. When they met in high school, Brian was easygoing and popular because he was friendly to everyone. Dom was a loner; his intense love for retro videogames and foreign movies was ahead of his time. They were partners in freshmen year chemistry and became inseparable friends, never looking back, even through the most brutal of fights.

He leaned into Chelsea and welcomed her embrace as he told himself there wasn't anything he could have done. Brian's fear for his own life exceeded whatever bond he and Dom had. He tried not to consider it an insult to their friendship, but something more base.

It was the only way his brain could make sense of it.

"I guess we should leave soon, too." Dom blinked away the forming tears in his eyes. "Let's try to rest and make a plan. Then we'll go."

"Can we make it on foot?" Chelsea said aloud.

"I don't know. The question is, do we want to?"

She paused, rubbing her fingers against her temples. "My friend Nina lives a few blocks away. She has a truck. If we could get to it, maybe we could all drive to the middle school?"

Dom nodded. "Yeah. That sounds good. I guess if this is a hoax, we'll know then. And we'll keep going."

"Hey?"

He looked up at her. She kissed him softly on the lips. "You did the right thing," she repeated. "You couldn't stop him."

"Then why does it feel like I sent him to his death?"

27 Dr. Marla Ainsworth

The eggs should've grown into larvae by now, but they hadn't. *They hadn't!*

It was definitive proof that her cure was going to work. Though she intended to ask for the assistance no matter what, she threatened Chandler and Suresh's lives if they ever tried to take credit for her work. Together they finished synthesizing a small batch of highly potent antihelminthics. What seemed like a deadly advantage to the parasite at first—its ability to exist in host blood long after exiting the body—was now working against it. They weren't racing against the clock to work with dying specimens.

They added the drug to the blood and watched as the organism consumed it.

After a day, the control sample without the drug showed the expected results; the parasite had grown into larvae. But the sample with her drug had not matured. It was nothing short of a miracle. The eggs were still alive, but they hadn't matured. It wasn't totally a cure, but it was the best thing they had. Having dormant eggs in the body was progress. They'd need to come up with a solution to kill the eggs off entirely to prevent flare-ups or resistance, but in the meantime what they had would work.

And the unsettling question of *why* and *how* the super powerful drug was working remained a mystery. It would remain that way until they had sufficient time to discover the specific mutation of Anisakis Nova. The danger in not knowing how her drug worked could be catastrophic, especially if the parasite developed resistance to it. Marla had to be satisfied in knowing an immediate stop to the spread would give them time to do that necessary research.

The three had been in the lab so long Marla wasn't sure what day it was. Mexican food and fretful sleep were a memory. The only bit of relief she had was comfort knowing the neighbor girl was feeding Doom twice a day. Even with the threat of humanity being wiped out, the girl still charged Marla a steep ten bucks a day that Marla wasn't there.

The three had been running tests to verify the results weren't a fluke, but it took precious time. The infection was approaching, the nation's panic level rising exponentially. That didn't make tests go any faster. But when she was satisfied they had a valid product, she sent a quick email off to Dr. Baker.

Shortly after that, the lab went into high alert. There was some kind of incident with one of the hosts on the other side of campus. Everyone was on lock down. Suresh insisted they remain in the lab until it was resolved.

Marla was frustrated. It interrupted their concentration and put everyone on edge. They hadn't gotten any work done in hours while they waited for security to give them the all clear.

She took the time to triple backup all her work, uploading it onto all of the work servers, uploading it to her external hard drive, and another encrypted flash drive she kept in her desk. She was midway through typing up the official findings to send to the entire CDC when Dr. Baker walked in the door.

28 Dom

It was barely dawn. The room was all dark shades of blue and black. He could barely make out Chelsea's pale face hovering above him.

After Brian left they stayed in the bathroom, taking their meals there and sleeping on and off. They'd tried staying in Dom's bedroom, but it didn't feel as safe as the windowless, enclosed space the bathroom offered.

Chelsea managed to call her friend, who agreed to the plan. Her boyfriend had left yesterday and never came back. She was alone and had planned on going to the evac zone anyway. If they could make it there in time, she'd take them with her.

Then people started fleeing. Dom was retrieving supplies from the storage room when he caught sight of them out the window. They passed the apartment in droves, carrying their children and luggage. The last time Dom checked before going to sleep they were shoulder to shoulder hustling down the road. He and Chelsea discussed leaving right then, but a fight erupted when a pack of infected started firing automatic assault rifles into the crowd from the strip mall roof. After that the street cleared out.

Across town were the sounds of a city falling. Wailing sirens. Gunshots. Screaming and shouting almost constantly. Military vehicles with giant speakers rolled by occasionally, telling citizens where the nearest evacuation zone was. That was all Dom and Chelsea needed for confirmation; the bombing wasn't a joke.

It was a wonder Dom managed to fall asleep at all; the exhaustion of it all was hitting him hard. The infected were dominating Seattle, their grip tight.

But that morning things seemed quieter. Whatever battle was being fought earlier was dying down. The brunt of evacuators was gone, making the area quiet. He'd be happy if it weren't for how unsettling it was. Silence had become uncommon.

"Dom, wake up," Chelsea whispered, nudging his shoulder. "Something is going on outside."

Waking up was the last thing he wanted to do, but he roused himself anyway. "What?"

"They have Brian."

Dom's mouth dried up and his heart skipped a beat. He was already shaking as he stumbled towards the window. He dropped to his knees and crawled to it, popping his head up just enough to see.

Brian had a noose around his neck, standing on the tailgate of a truck. The rope was tied to the stoplight pole above him. It changed from red to green, casting the entire crowd gathering around them in an unearthly light. The crazies set up fires in trashcans close to the strip mall. A convoy of cars that hadn't been there before were parked in the road and all over the parking lot.

Down the street the sun was just peeking over the edge of the horizon. The mass of infected swayed against each other, their faces turned towards Brian. They were waiting for something.

A man crawled on top of the cab of the truck. He was naked, most of his body covered in something. Dom wondered if it was blood, but it was too hard to tell in the light. He pushed the window up just slightly so he could hear.

"Everyone!" He spread his arms wide. His right arm began jerking backwards wildly. He grabbed it and steadied

121

it with his left. "We were gathered here today to join thisssss fella with one of our own beautiful ladiesssss." The man had a hard time moving on from the S sound in his sentences. He slapped his jaw violently when he landed on them until he managed to move to the next word.

"Carl, bring out a lady!"

Two men led a pregnant woman out from the sports store in the strip mall. It wasn't until she came closer that Dom realized she was infected with the parasite and ready to burst, like the guy on the news said. Her back was arched so far back her arms dangled behind her, head lolled back, her distended stomach leading the way.

"Now, thissss lady was ready to give her love to thissss guy. But he sssaid no." The man shook his head so hard Dom thought it would snap. "Not okay. We're going to make him pay for it 'causss thisss girl iss ready to pop!"

The men positioned her in front of him. One pulled a machete from the back of the truck. He poised it over her stomach.

"God, please help me!"

"No God helping you now. I'm going to give you once lassst chance. You want her or not?"

"You're fucking sick!"

Brian's voice cut across the street. Dom ducked below the window, dragging Chelsea with him. "Don't look," he whispered.

It was silent, then they heard the first howl. He peeked over the edge, compelled to make sure it was all really happening.

Worms crawled up Brian's body. They converged at his mouth, working their way into his body. Their slick forms caught the rising sunlight and glittered in bodily fluids and slime. Blood spurted from everywhere where they entered his body. It began flowing from his mouth as they ate through him.

Dom bit the flesh of his palm to stop his own scream welling in his throat. The group of infected jumped in glee, jostling each other and laughing.

He wrapped his arms around Chelsea as the world came crashing down around him.

He finally realized he might not make it out alive.

***

They spent the rest of the day praying the crowd outside would disperse, giving them a chance to escape and make a run for Nina's. They had less than a day left to make it to the middle school.

Chelsea wanted to talk about what happened to Brian. Why was it that whenever he did want to talk about something, she didn't? Then the second he needed to not think, she was all over him. The only way he could think to come to terms with what he'd seen was to first ignore it until the memory wasn't so raw. She wanted to analyze it, replay it over and over until it wasn't anything anymore.

The day stretched on in silence for Chelsea and Dom, but outside the crazies were in the throes of a wild party. The mixture of frantic glee and painful screaming was unbearable. Dom peeked outside just once. After catching a glimpse of a gang rape, he vowed not to look again until the noise stopped.

"Here." Chelsea handed him a bag of chips. They were still sequestering themselves in the bathroom. Dom suspected they couldn't really see them from street level in the apartment anyway, but he didn't want to risk it. He took the chips, setting them on the floor beside him. "Thanks."

"What happened wasn't your fault."

"I told you I don't want to talk about this."

"I know you said that. I—"

"For fuck's sake, Chelsea! You don't care that Brian is gone. You're happy he's dead. You hated him. Stop trying to console me about it. It's obvious you're smug about it and that's the last thing I need right now."

Her mouth snapped shut. She stared at the towel rack. "I'm sorry."

Dom felt his lip quiver. He pressed his hand against his mouth and blinked away the tears. "You should be."

Her hand was gentle against his leg. She pulled him down, cradling him in her arms. "We're going to forget everything that's happened up to now. We're going to wait for the right moment and we're getting out of here. We're going to get to the evacuation stop where guys with big guns who know how to use them will protect us."

She kissed the top of his head. "We're going to be okay."

"I know. But I just keep thinking about what I could've said to stop him. Or about how naïve we all were, thinking we could hole up in the apartment and wait it out. You can't wait out the end of the world."

"We couldn't know this was going to happen," she said. "We had a good setup. Brian cracked under pressure. I didn't help any. Being cooped up in this apartment gave us all cabin fever. We've all been scared and at each other's throats."

"I haven't," Dom countered. He had been wrong about one thing; he did want to talk. He felt a heaviness begin lifting off his chest the more he hashed things out with Chelsea. "I've been peacekeeping between you two."

"You know in the movies how one person ends up being the leader?"

"Yeah."

"That's you. But you're so busy trying to keep the peace between people, you don't see what's happening right in front of you. You don't see the breakdown of our group. Brian was cracking on day two. I've been on the verge of a breakdown from day one. Meanwhile you've been treating us like kids and, well, it enables us to keep acting like it."

"We're all at fault," Dom said, both a question and a statement.

"We are."

They sat in silence, each of them mulling over the past week. Then Dom perked up, listening. It *was* silent. No more party outside.

He crawled to the window and looked out just in time to see two cars rumble to life and drive away. The group was gone, leaving the strip mall and street barren of life. Smoke wafted from the trashcan bonfires. Dead bodies, mutilated in all forms, were scattered about, evidence of their debauchery.

"Chelsea, let's go. Now."

She came from the bathroom and looked out the window. Without another word they donned their gear and left the apartment.

29 Sadie

Jon was infected. Her little boy was infected. Sadie wore a scarf wrapped around her mouth and nose so she could sit by him and stomach the smell. Jon laid on his back, his bare chest glistening with sweat. She'd given up on wiping away the viscous liquid, since it seemed to come back within moments. She watched the tiny worms crawling just underneath his skin.

If she had just kept a better eye on him. If she had done *anything*.,,

The town was going to be bombed soon. She packed a bag with some essentials for her and Jon. She knew the basics of using the revolver the neighbor's girlfriend left her, but she wasn't confident. Sadie hoped she wouldn't have to use it.

She wasn't going to leave Jon behind, even though he was sick. Sadie planned on skirting past the evacuation zones and ferrying him to safety. They'd find somewhere she could restrain him and keep him safe until the government came up with a cure.

They would, wouldn't they? Someone had to figure it out.

She wasn't sure how long he had left until he woke up, but she couldn't risk him hurting himself or her if he did before they escaped. She used her phone charger cable and some kitchen twine to bind his hands and his feet. Her tears dripped onto his tiny form as she carried him down the stairs. The neighbors blocked off the exits, but she climbed through a window in the main office. Sadie hoped the night would make it hard for the crazy people to see her.

He was easy to carry at first, but soon the weight became difficult. She frequently took breaks, resting behind dumpsters or just inside buildings.

The few miles she had to walk started to seem impossible. She was tired from sleepless nights in the apartment, her nerves fried from being so cautious.

She stroked Jon's face. He growled in his sleep. Her hand reflexively snapped back, the action making her feel ashamed. Somewhere nearby a man was yelling for a new hen and making terrible crowing noise. Sadie picked up Jon, ignoring the burning pain in her arms, and kept pressing forward.

30 Adam

Adam fled the scene right when the first guard went down, heading straight for his office on reflex. He anticipated a barrage of security at his office, but as he exited the elevator and headed down his hall, there was no one. They hadn't had time to review the security footage and peg the situation on Adam. Then again, it *was* his fault, but would they arrive to that conclusion based on what they saw?

He flipped the lock on the door as he imagined insane, infected people coming for him. The white worms slithering down the hallway after him.

Deep breath. Breathe, you aren't breathing.

As he tried to calm himself down he flicked on his computer and pulled up the video feed for the host retaining rooms. After clicking through, he finally found the mess he was looking for.

Two new guards were on the ground in the host room, their bodies crawling with worms. Adam flicked to the viewing room. Another handful of guards were gesturing wildly, obviously unsure of what to do.

No one could help anyone. If one batch of worms from a host was powerful enough to take out three guards, it wasn't surprising how the parasite was taking over like wildfire. Adam pressed his fingertips against his cheek.

It wasn't surprising at all.

"Oh God, listen to yourself," Adam groaned to his empty office. "This isn't about you!"

He accessed security from the rest of the host storage buildings. All the night security was rushing towards the scene. They were all distracted. Everyone seemed to have forgotten about Adam Baker, the cause of it all. That was why no one came for him. In fact, they might not even know he'd been there.

But they would. Eventually. Once they reviewed the footage and audio recordings in the room, they'd know Adam's involvement.

Adam's mind raced as he desperately tried to weave an excuse for what he did. He hoped his boss would see the necessary logic in trying to prevent the host from killing himself. He had a whole spiel about it. Damage control, he thought.

But as he replayed the events in his head, there was no getting around it. He messed up and two guards—the number rising—were dead because of it. Those men were gone because of his scientific inclinations. He blamed it on sleeplessness, desperation, and an overstressed mind.

Worst of all, he might be infected himself. Adam dug his first aid kit from his bottom desk drawer and doused the wound on his cheek with alcohol and put a Band-Aid on it. It stung as though the worm were still in it. The hole was circular, the ends slightly ragged from where it's little teeth tore away. It was already puckering, looking infected and yellowed.

His daughters watched him from a photo on his desk. Disneyland for their eighth birthdays. Should he call them? Say goodbye while he was still himself?

No. It would scare them. If they even cared.

He wasn't sure how to proceed. It was obvious he'd gotten out of hand. With the pressure to come up with answers and his own desire to understand the parasite, he let himself do something a normal person wouldn't do. Put someone else's life in jeopardy for his own benefit.

Adam collapsed into his desk chair, the reality of his terrible situation fully sinking in. He ran through the stages of infection, imagining himself in each. Would he be an adequate host for full maturation of the parasite? Would he be like Sam Price?

His stomach grumbled. His head was beginning to ache and he saw a fuzzy aura around the computer screen and desk lamp that reminded him of when he had a bad migraine. He wondered if it was from stress or if it was a symptom. He'd be lying to himself if he thought the former.

A chiming sound drew his attention to his computer. His email flashed; one new message.

Dr. Baker, we think we might have come up with a potential vaccination. Please come to lab ASAP. Marla.

Vaccination? His heart fluttered with hope. Adam raised his hands to type a response when he felt a wave of dizziness sweep over him. He braced himself against the desk as he leaned over and vomited. It splashed against his shoes and made a garish brown stain on the tan carpet.

The world spun around him. He slid from his chair, landing in his own vomit, and slumped onto his side as everything went black around him.

***

Through the darkness of his subconscious, the memories of his life projected in his dreams in a long feverish sequence.

Growing up, no one understood him. They always stopped him from doing what he wanted, which was to stay indoors and read. When he was a teenager his father was ashamed of his bookworm son who was entirely uninterested in sports, the family mechanic business, or anything stereotypically masculine. Both his older and younger brother called him a faggot; he'd heard his father stifle chuckles at his siblings' tormenting jokes.

His mother was nowhere to be found. Not because she wasn't there; she was. Instead, she was a ghost in their lives, feeding them and doing chores, sending them off to school with all the right supplies. Providing sympathetic nods or coos to everyone's woes. But she wasn't a real person to anyone in the family. Adam saw her in his memories as a statue, worn and tired, at the stove, at the washer and dryer. Always tucking a Kleenex into her front cardigan pocket and eyeing Adam with unspoken regret.

High school passed by. Girls thought he was cute—he heard them whispering—but everyone thought he was weird even though they couldn't place why. Adam didn't know why, either. He just had a deep interest in science and how things worked. That was the source of endless harassment and bullying. Being smart was something to be ashamed of.

The early adult years. The extensive college years. Memories of exams he did poorly on, or awkward and painful social encounters, were heightened. He remembered every detail of being kicked out of a theoretical debate team on genetic modification because of his "outlandish and disturbing" ideas. Getting his lab internships, working the job of his dreams.

His marriage. The job at the CDC that was politics and deskwork.

And Gina. That fucking bitch. That harlot who destroyed his entire life because she wanted a free ride of her own. That dimwitted woman who tore him away from his beloved Seattle, from his friends, from *everything*.

His memories brought him to the very moment when he told the guard to go in. When the parasite began burrowing into him.

And now.

Adam's eyes flickered open. Before him was a view of under his desk. A mess of thick dust and computer cords.

Around his body the carpet was saturated with sweat. His sweat. He registered the smell and knew it was his defense mechanism sweat.

Blades of sunlight cut through the room. Had he been out the night? Two nights?

It was the right thing to do, sending the guard in. The host might not have burst otherwise. But at the same time, it was wrong. Wrong only because he could've been caught. Because he hadn't been smart about it. Because...

The parasite was giving him a chance to reinvent himself. After this—if there was going to *be* an after this— everything would be different. A new world was brewing. One he wanted to be in control of, doing what he wanted when he wanted.

Fuck his wife, fuck his old life. He repeated the words in a sing-song voice, enjoying how they sounded.

Incoherent thoughts kept pulsing in and out. His brain wanted to think about the past, present, and future all at once. It made him feel disoriented, sick from the overwhelming amount of things to think about. He slapped his hand against his forehead in attempt to stave off the agitated slew of thoughts, but none subsided.

He became vaguely aware that he was infected. The thought was distant, tucked away in his mind like a memory he had to recollect, but it was there. The parasite was inside of him, but it didn't seem so bad. Set aside the frantic ideas and aching body, he felt quite like himself.

Didn't he?

Adam pushed himself to his feet and paced around the room. Waves of anger and confusion swept over him so violently his body reared against it. He was himself, but not himself. At one moment he had control over his thoughts, the next, horrific images plagued him.

Strangling Gina and stringing her body up over her beloved mid-century coffee table they paid an outrageous amount for. Cut out those eyes that were always looking at him like he wasn't enough.

Making his daughters beg for mercy as he skinned them, reupholstering the front seat of the car with their skin.

Burning everyone on campus alive, one by one, and smelling their meat as it burnt to a crisp.

Adam braced himself against a wall, panting. That little part of him saying those thoughts were wrong was quickly fading. In fact, it felt very good to relish in those images. The notion of giving in to his base desires was intensely desirable.

A series of knocks on the door drew his attention. "Dr. Baker? This is security, please open the door."

They were here. They blamed him. They found him out.

Kill them, rip them up. Feel their blood.

The urge came over him so strongly he knew he had to satiate it.

"I'm coming," Adam found himself saying. His voice sounded even, to his own surprise. It didn't match the rising rage within. "Is everything okay?"

"We want to make sure you're okay after last night. Please open the door."

Adam scanned his office. He spotted a heavy glass award he'd received years ago for—what for? He couldn't remember. As he hefted it into his hands he knew it would get the job done.

"I'm hurt. My leg."

He positioned himself by the door. He heard the beep of the guard's universal security card, then his door clicking as it unlocked itself. Adam hadn't considered there being more than one, but lucky for him, it was just the one.

The first blow knocked him to the ground. The sharp corner of the award crushed a neat dent into his skull.

Blood spurted wildly over the floor and wall. His body convulsed.

Adam brought the bludgeoning device down over and over until his arms felt tired and there wasn't anything left of the security guard's skull but pulpy brain and fragments of bone.

He felt good. He felt *alive*. Everyone should feel like this, Adam thought. Before the parasite got him, the infection was spreading with alarming speed. Now it wasn't going fast enough. Could it be stronger? Could incubation times be reduced? There was much to learn.

He turned and faced his office. His gaze fell onto his computer. The email Marla sent last night...a vaccination...

Vaccination? Cure? That was bad. That meant he couldn't do what he wanted to. All the new budding dreams he had of experimentation, killing, and being true to his desires would be gone.

No, that must be put to a stop. To maintain his freedom from the constraints of bureaucracy and morals there couldn't be anything stopping the infection from spreading. Didn't anyone understand the beauty and complexity of its design? How it was freeing the world from whatever burdened them?

This is what he was meant for. That grand thing he'd been waiting for his entire life. It wasn't God or the paranormal. It was a little white worm that ate people from the inside out, that gave others the ability to be truly free.

His daughters' faces again. He picked up the photo and threw it across the room, the glass and frame shattering against the wall. He didn't have to regret the past two decades. Now he could do what he wanted. He'd go back to Seattle, where he'd wanted to be his entire life, and start anew. And, to make it all even better, he knew what his topic of interest would be upon arrival. The parasite. Anything and everything to do with it.

Here it was; Adam Baker's Big Break.

He began printing his reports and notes, shoving them into his briefcase. It would all help him launch his own research and experimentation once he found a good place to settle in. Would his old apartment still be there? Adam supposed it wouldn't matter if it was inhabited. He'd kill whoever was there.

After packing all his files, he reoriented. He needed to destroy anything Marla had developed on a potential vaccination. That meant backups, copies, and knowing who she spoke to about it. He didn't know how far she was into developing it, so he had to act fast and put a stop to it. Marla was bright, very smart indeed; could she be useful in his own research?

A thought came to him. Infect Marla. Make her like him so she could help him. He'd admired how bright and clever she was in the lab recently.

Would semen pass the parasite onto her? He grinned. Probably.

Before he left, he searched the guard. He carried a nice handgun on his hip. Adam studied the gun. The brand was Glock. He didn't know much about guns, but he knew that was a popular brand. He remembered what his brother always said: Glocks don't have safeties. You're the safety.

Rupert. He was going to kill Rupert when he got back to Seattle.

Adam tore down the curtains and tried toweling off as much of the sweat as he could. Now that he was infected himself, the smell wasn't bad. It was almost sweet and earthy. He made a mental note to consider this further once he had time.

Gun stuffed in the waistband of his pants, he tried to steady his breathing and look normal as he walked about the halls. They were vacant. Perhaps it was too early in the morning? Or had everyone abandoned ship? How long was he asleep for?

He entered the elevator to the lab level and leaned against the wall. He was racing against the clock. Someone would come looking for the guard he killed—that was technically his third kill, he'd say—and then they'd be looking for him.

He found himself laughing. Little did they know he wasn't the same Adam anymore. Not the demure little scientist who put his head down and worked. Not the Adam who let his bitch wife control him.

31 Gary

The new girl struggled harder than any of the others had. When he plucked her away from her idiotic boyfriend, she elbowed him in the nose and darted forward with every bit of strength she had. If she wanted to go with him, why was she being a little bitch? Putting up such a fight?

But it wasn't enough to stop Gary. No, he was determined to have her. Back in the coop, all but Heather were big-bellied and ready to burst. Heather awoke from her coma and was crazy, screaming about sawing his cock off with a nail file, so he had to kill her. He'd barely have any girls left in his coop after the other ladies exploded.

He'd heard the guy call his new girl Chelsea, but that wasn't a good name. He wanted to call her Christine Ruth. It sounded like a very fancy name for a very beautiful girl. It was the name of his first and last girl before he went to Greenwood.

Christine Ruth struggled, but not enough. He got his arm around her neck and held it tight until her little body sagged and she fell unconscious. They hadn't wandered far from the strip mall, so dragging her back didn't take long. Just as he was tying her up to one of the chairs, she woke.

Gary felt heat spreading across his groin. She really was beautiful. Even as she came to and started screaming, he noticed how delicate her pink tongue was. Her perfect white teeth.

She kicked at him wildly but he caught her legs and straddled them, leaning in close. "I've been watching you, pretty lady. I thought you would be a good fit in the coop. Join the rest of my hens."

Silence overtook her as she followed his gaze deeper into the salon where his other ladies laid in a row, their stomachs distended, ready to burst thousands of parasites into the world.

"Please let me go."

Gary frowned. "I can't do that."

"Why? Please just let me go!"

He crawled up her body, one hand sliding up her side. "Because you're mine now, pretty girl. Pretty Christine Ruth, so pretty—"

Something hard pressed against the back of his head.

"Get your fucking hands off her."

Gary got to his feet and slowly turned. It was Christine Ruth's boyfriend holding a shotgun to his head.

"Hey now," Gary said, putting on his regular person voice. "Nothing wrong here. Just keeping the girls, you know. These hens need a lot of maintenance."

Surely the boyfriend would understand he was just doing the best for them? Gary was just a regular guy doing his thing. Gary was a nice guy.

"The fuck is wrong with you? You—"

Gary saw his chance. The boyfriend spotted the girls laying in the back and was distracted. He lunged forward, pushing the barrel of the gun upward as he knocked him back.

There wasn't room for another rooster in this nest.

32 Dom

When Dom realized Chelsea was no longer with him, his heart stopped. The world spun around him and he wasn't sure what to do. As he scanned the street behind him he didn't know where she could've gone or why she left him.

He took a few steps forward and felt his knees weaken. He set his hand against the alley wall for support and took deep breaths. Dom needed to focus. If he didn't, there was no way he could find Chelsea.

Outside was overwhelming him. In the apartment everything was slow, so much so that every decision they made was agonizing. Now he felt like he was moving in fast forward. The smell of smoke, blood, and sour rot was overpowering. The sight of complete devastation on street level disoriented him.

Sensory overload, his mind kept repeating.

One street over he heard a series of shrill screams and the popping of an automatic rifle. Dom decided backtracking was the best way to begin looking for her. As he neared the end of the alley, he caught sight of movement headed towards the strip mall. A man was dragging Chelsea's unconscious body across the street. He was obviously one of the infected crazies.

Although he was making good speed, he seemed to have no control of his limbs, which jerked as though being tugged. But what worried Dom the most was the shotgun he had slung across his back.

If he saw Dom he might kill Chelsea, or him. He needed to sneak up on him. Dom waited until the man dragged Chelsea into a salon then crept in after him, working his way around dead bodies littering the street. It took all the willpower he had not to run screaming and guns blazing to her.

When he slipped into the salon, he feared he wouldn't be able to take the man. Fortunately he was distracted, his hands all over Chelsea, and it gave Dom ample time to get right behind him and point his own gun at his head.

Everything was going fine until the infected stood and lunged at Dom. Dom did his best to push the guy away, but he was bigger. His shotgun went upward, but he didn't lose grip of it. He sidestepped and let the man's momentum ram him into a rack of beauty products. They tumbled around him as he fell.

Dom brought the shotgun back up and aimed.

"Shoot him! Kill him!"

He stopped thinking. He squeezed the trigger. The infected man's head exploded in a burst of gore that splattered everything behind him, mixing with burst shampoo bottles as it dripped. Dom watched in rapt horror as tiny white worms, no bigger than his pinky nail, squirmed about in the mess.

"Help." Her voice was faint. Dom spun and dropped to his knees, pulling out a knife from his pocket to cut Chelsea free.

"Are you okay?" Dom said, trying to still his shaking hands as he cut through. "Did he hurt you?"

"No. I'm okay."

As the ties came free he saw her raw, scraped wrists. Her neck looked bruised. But she was putting her strong face on and right then, Dom needed her to be strong for the both of them. He helped her to her feet.

She stared at the motionless body of the crazy man and stepped back. "Dom, those worms are crawling towards us," she whispered.

They were. Slowly, since they were so small, the worms were migrating towards them. Dom took Chelsea's hand and gave it a squeeze. "It's fine. We're out of here, back on our way to Nina's. We've still got hours left. We're good."

"Where you going?"

Chelsea and Dom turned towards a voice from the back of the salon. A naked woman stepped forward. Her stomach was so far distended she had to lean backward to support its weight. Though dark, Dom spotted other women behind her, all of them infected with the parasite and ready to explode.

"Don't you want to have a good time with us?"

Dom spotted the scissors in her hand. He remembered what he'd read about and seen. Hosts wanted to spread the parasite. Before the word *run* even slipped his mouth, the woman pierced the scissors into the middle of her stomach. It split like an overfilled water balloon, the wave of bloody, eager parasites within bursting forward.

These worms were bigger. They were faster. And as the other women tore their infected bodies open, there were more of them.

Dom turned and ran for the door, dragging Chelsea behind him. He felt debris pelting his back then he realized one of the women exploded close by. It was worms hitting him.

Outside even the overcast sky blinded them after the dimness of the salon. He was disoriented for a moment before deciding to resume the original plan. Only now they were being pursued and it wasn't going to be easy.

Behind them a mass of worms slithered towards them. Two women who hadn't burst themselves followed, their bodies moving disturbingly quick considering their size. Drawn by the commotion, a handful of people came from the sports store next door, men wearing what appeared to

141

be human flesh as loincloths. They each carried pipes and baseball bats.

Dom took it all in with once glance. He aimed his shotgun and took out the nearest threat—one of the salon women—whose stomach exploded upon impact against the cement.

They booked it towards the apartment, taking a sharp turn as they entered the alley.

"He took my gun!" Chelsea shouted, almost breathless, as they ran.

Dom reached into his holster and gave her his sidearm, a feeling of hopelessness overcoming him. Not thirty minutes out of the apartment and they were already fucked.

But there were maybe five of the flesh-wearers and one woman left. If they made a stand...

His ears rang as he lost his hearing from the shot Chelsea fired without warning by his side. She'd hit the host in the shoulder. She took aim again and fired, the round hitting her in the middle of the chest. Dom watched in horror as the woman kept coming, a tear in the bullet hole traveling downward until her stomach finally split open, a gush of parasites falling onto the ground and joining the ranks of the others.

The people they could kill. The parasites? He took aim at the mass and fired. The buckshot was absorbed into the parasites. They bled, but kept coming.

They were at the point where Dom lost Chelsea before. When they first left the apartment it seemed doable to walk down the back alleys until they reached Chelsea's friend's apartment. His hearing was jacked from the gunshots; everything sounded like he was underwater. His hands trembled, the reality of killing people threatening to shut him down.

Stop. Stop doubting yourself. You have *to do this.*

Dom stopped, turned, and fired at the oncoming infected instead of the parasites. He hit one of them square in the chest. He crumpled to the ground. There were four left, the parasites moving quickly across the cement ten yards away.

Dom cocked the gun, aimed, and fired again. Another hit. Chelsea joined, hitting one in the leg, effectively bringing him down.

The remaining two veered behind a building. Whether they were trying to cut them off or had given up, Dom wasn't sure. But they were gone. Without a word they kept going down the alley, darting across a side street as they reentered on the other side.

His chest was on fire. Phlegm was thick in his throat from running so hard after being sedentary for so long. Though the parasites were fast moving—and horrifying in close quarters—out in the open they were slowed down by debris, wrecked cars, and dead bodies. As they turned a corner and Dom checked again, he realized the mass of parasites was nowhere to be seen.

"How close are we?"

Chelsea studied her surroundings. "One block. We're behind the Thai place Nina and I usually eat at."

Eventually they arrived at the back of a small apartment building, very similar to Dom's. It was six stories and only one building. Giant dumpsters reeked of old garbage. Dom breathed through his mouth but the smell still got him.

Chelsea flicked out her cell phone and gave Nina a call. No one answered. Dom tried the backdoor. Locked. There was a security pad by the door, but Chelsea didn't know the number to get in.

"Do we break in?" he whispered.

"We have to. We either go on foot or try to get the keys to her truck."

Dom knew he'd seen people do techniques in the movies to make glass breaking less loud, but every one of them escaped him. Really, it was just his mind being overactive. He focused and took the butt of his gun and broke the panel closest to the doorknob. The sound sent panic coursing through his body. He reached through and opened the door.

They slid in, checking the hallway for threats. Glass crunched underfoot. There was no one in sight. To their right was a long wall of mailboxes, to their left a communal area and leasing office.

"Second floor, just around the corner," Chelsea said.

They took the stairs by the elevator. Dom kept an eye behind them as Chelsea tapped on Nina's door.

"Something's wrong. The door is open." She raised her handgun and pushed the door open while Dom pointed his gun into the opening.

Ten feet into the living room Nina lay on her back, her chest heaving but otherwise motionless. A sickly, sour scent hit Dom. He gagged, taking a step back and putting the edge of his jacket against his nose.

Yellow sweat pooled around her onto the tiled floor. Circular, bloody wounds were all over her arms and legs where her skin was exposed. Her eyelids were red, veins darkening as they spiraled outward. The worms got her. Were they still in the apartment? What had happened?

Dom spotted a key bowl on an end table by Nina. A set of keys was still in it. He kept his gun on her body as he went past Chelsea to pick them up. The closer he got, the more unbearable the scent. His eyes watered as he pocketed the keys.

Whatever happened to Nina, there was nothing they could do now.

They closed the door behind them. Chelsea's expression was neutral. Dom didn't say a thing about her friend. "We get outside and run straight for the truck. The nearest evac zone is only a ten minute drive away."

He took her hand in his and gave it a hard squeeze. "We're going to make it."

33 Adam

The guard's blood felt sticky on Adam's hands, almost dried but still a bit tacky. Marla was silent in the passenger's side of his car, but he knew she was crying. He wanted to lick up her tears and cut her eyes out all at the same time.

Getting Marla didn't go off without a hitch. Well, at first it did. He entered the lab and saw her. Two other techs were there. When she saw him she gasped.

"Dr. Baker! Are you okay? We heard there was a breach last night. Four guards dead. They didn't get it under control until just a few hours ago. Burned every last parasite from the male host specimen *and* the bodies."

"I'm okay," he assured her. "I felt so sickened by the whole incident, I went to my office and collapsed from shock. But I'm fine now."

"You...hey, what's wrong with your eyes?"

Adam blinked. He wiped at his eyes and his fingers came away reddish. The hosts always had bloody eyes, a symptom of the parasite. He'd forgotten about it.

That's when he raised his gun and killed both the techs. He shot Marla in the leg as she was trying to escape. The bullet only grazed her. Nothing she'd die from. They'd bandage it up later and she'd be fine.

But his hardships didn't end there. Before Adam exited the lab, he saw a guard booking it down the hall. He turned to Marla. "Stay here. If you move a muscle, I'll cut your fucking tongue out and make you eat it. Got it?" She answered with a single nod.

Adam decided on trying to play it cool to get the upper hand. He walked down the hallway and nodded as he approached. Casual. Be casual. "Just checking on some lab results. I'm Dr. Baker." He flashed his badge.

That's when the guard raised his gun and told Adam to lay face down on the floor.

Adam feigned kneeling and withdrew his gun. The guard hadn't expected it. Three bullets later and he was on the ground, blood pooling around his dead figure. Adam grabbed the guard's security card, weapons, and handcuffs, his hands glossing over hot, blood covered clothing. The coppery scent made him hungry and excited. The erection pressing against his pants, elicited by the raw violence of the encounter, felt better than anything he'd experienced before.

And Marla? Marla was crying, begging for her life as he made her gather up specimens and pack them in a case. He held the gun to her head as he watched her delete file after file of data on the parasite. It felt good to be in control of everyone around him. The gun made everything so much easier.

Guns were good. Guns made people he didn't want around go away. He needed more of them, and as soon as possible.

Halfway to the parking garage, the hallway emergency lights began flashing. It meant the entire building was on red alert. Total shut down. Adam reveled in the thought of more idiotic soldiers being infected by the worms, by his brethren spreading it further.

The whole building was probably going to be infected before the night was over.

He shoved Marla into the front seat and handcuffed her right hand to the door, taking a moment to breathe in her scent as he leaned over her to buckle her in. No sense in getting her killed in a car crash after coming this far.

After he peeled out of the parking garage, he headed straight for the airport only to find the state of Georgia had grounded all incoming and outgoing air travel. Part of him expected he wouldn't be flying, but not because air travel was restricted. He'd pictured something much more movie-like. That the government blocked his identification and credit cards, stopping him from flying. Or S.W.AT. was waiting.

Then the whole idea was bad. What was he thinking? He tried shaking the cobwebs out of his head. Stupid. Stupid fucking idea to take a plane. He caught his reflection in the rearview mirror. His eyes were indeed bloody, his complexion pallid, and he had a wildness about him that would alert airport security.

"Fuck!" he screamed, banging his hands against the steering wheel until they throbbed in pain. He pressed his body back against the seat and took in a ragged breath. It was difficult to make his body behave. "We're driving, I guess."

"Adam…"

"Shut your mouth, bitch. And it's still Dr. Baker to you. At least until we start getting more friendly with each other."

The sobs began and, since she wouldn't stop, Adam removed his tie and shoved it in her mouth. Unlike the movies, it didn't work. She spit it back out. He tied it tightly around her head instead, which seemed to work better.

He used the built in GPS in his car to make a route to Seattle. Instead of skirting around infected areas, he opted to go straight through them as all the traffic cameras showed lanes heading inward almost empty. Everyone was leaving. No one was going in.

After an hour of driving he needed to get gas. Before he pulled into the station he removed Marla's gag and told her if she screamed or tried to get anyone's attention, he'd kill anyone who saw.

"Not you, though. I'll keep you around and make you *suffer* for trying."

She did as he said. In fact, she behaved so well he took the time to go into the convenience store to buy snacks. He kept an eye on her the entire time as he gathered armfuls of chips and candy. She never moved. Good girl.

Keeping his eyes down, he dumped the pile at the cash register and retrieved his wallet. But he'd noticed the cashier's dark, tinted glasses.

"Kind of strange to wear sunglasses inside," Adam remarked, clutching a fifty note in his hand.

"Transition lenses. I thought they'd be great, but after a while they never transitioned back. Can't afford to get new ones though, since I lost my job and started working at this dump."

When the new Adam wanted something, he got it. Adam smiled, reaching into his pants for his gun.

34 Dr. Marla Ainsworth

Marla cursed God for the first few hours. She cried. She tried reasoning with her capturer. She passed in and out of darkness from the pain in her leg, so unbearable at times she was sure she was on the verge of death. It was some terrible cosmic joke that she was so close to a cure when it was taken away from her.

She kept her eyes closed, unwilling to look at the man. How long until Dr. Baker killed her? How long until she bled out or died from infection? Would he spread the infection to her? What would it feel like?

It wasn't until he stopped the car at the gas station that she finally opened her eyes and looked at him. Or, more specifically, the cell phone in the console.

She'd been so disoriented and afraid before, she hadn't done the one thing she knew how to do best; think. Analyze. When Dr. Baker told her to be quiet, she complied. All she needed to do was contact someone, anyone, and tell them where she was, to come save her...

The thought died there. Marla was as good as gone. No one would be able to save her. She didn't know where she was or where she was going. Emergency services would undoubtedly be swamped with more pressing matters.

What she needed to do was tell someone about her work. Someone who could *do* something and fast. This wasn't about her name in the books anymore. This wasn't about proving her worth.

This was about saving humanity.

Marla waited until Dr. Baker was in the building to grab the cell phone. This time she thanked God it was still charged, that Dr. Baker hadn't cuffed both her hands, that he left her alone. She kept perfectly still in case he was watching her from inside the store.

She tried calling Eskilson. It went straight to voicemail. She looked at the next number on his outgoing. It was to Barry. It rang and rang, finally going to voicemail. Marla didn't have time to keep trying people.

"Barry, this is Dr. Marla Ainsworth. I found a cure, but there is only one copy of my research in the flash drive in my second desk drawer. The password is Doom—I'm not joking. D-O-O-M. It works. It will save us. Baker has me hostage, he's infected. Please, Barry, please make sure someone takes care of my cat…"

She heard a gunshot from the convenience store and hung up, placing the phone exactly where she found it, hoping Barry wasn't dead. That she hadn't wasted her last words for nothing.

35 Dom

For the first time in days Dom felt his spirit lift.

After they pulled onto the main drag leading to the middle school, the scene improved. Military vehicles and soldiers were at every block. Droves of people walked beside cars that made slow progress. The sun was setting, but they'd set up floodlights everywhere to ensure the path was bright.

Dom hated thinking of all the people stuck in their homes, like he'd been not long ago, wondering how they could escape. Seeing the infected outside and feeling like they were going to die. The sense of bleak hopelessness ate away at you quicker than you expected it to.

As the street became more congested it became impossible to drive. He gradually pulled the truck off to the side of the street. The people on foot were making far better time than they were anyway. He began pushing the truck door open, but Chelsea stopped him.

"Our guns?"

Dom looked at his shotgun and her handgun, then to the crowd outside. No one had any weapons that he could see. Either they didn't have any—Seattle was a very liberal area—or they were keeping them hidden. Dom didn't want to part with the shotgun, but there wasn't a good way to hide it. He worried other survivors would see it and attempt to take it. It wouldn't take many of them to overwhelm him.

"We take the handguns. Hide it in the pack, okay?"

She nodded.

They exited the car and joined the mass of nervous people making their way to the evac point. His pack bumped into people, who either snapped at him or were too afraid to say anything. The military guys had their guns on the ready, scanning the crowd.

They rounded a corner and saw a soldier manning a machine gun on a Humvee in the middle of the road. The road was a T, the middle school at its conjunction, and the blockade appeared to be a funneling point before people entered the school. A barricade had been set up, forcing people to exit their vehicles if they had one and go on foot. Dom was glad they'd dropped the truck earlier, because the military was paying extra close attention to vehicles that made it that far.

Behind the Humvee, two pathways had been created out of fences. They were narrow, only allowing lines two people wide to go in at a time.

The lights were blinding. Dogs were barking. Guns were pointed. Dom began to feel uneasy. He took Chelsea's hand and followed behind a mother and daughter.

"Please walk slowly. When you arrive at Gate 1 you will be checked for signs of the parasite." The soldier with the horn shouting commands stood near Gate 1, gesturing people through. "The buses will be arriving soon. When you reach Gate 2, you'll be assigned a room to wait in at the middle school until further notice!"

The daughter in front of them started to cry. "Mom, I thought you said we were getting on the bus right away?"

She gripped her daughter's coat, pulling her closer. "Shhh. It's going to be okay."

After being funneled into one of the pathways they arrived at Gate 1, which was actually just a wider, fenced off space with more soldiers and guys in hazmat suits. A coffee shop on the left side of the street looked like a makeshift headquarters where soldiers and other official looking people were set up.

Dom turned his attention to what was in front of him. People were being taken one by one behind curtained areas in the Gate 1 section.

This was normal, Dom told himself. They had to do this to make sure only healthy people made it to the evacuation zones. But they weren't going fast enough considering Seattle was going to be bombed in only a few hours.

Behind them a slew of gunshots went off. The crowd ducked simultaneously. All of the soldiers' walkie talkies crackled to life. *"1 infected on perimeter of entry. Threat eliminated."*

Dom gripped Chelsea's hand and gave her his best reassuring look even though anxiety was creeping up his chest, constricting his breath and speeding up his pulse. A spot opened up. A soldier came and nodded at Dom and told him to follow. As the soldier pulled the curtain aside and shoved him in, he saw Chelsea go into the one next to him.

Then the questions, first from the soldier as a doctor-like figure yanked up Dom's sleeves and began checking his arms.

"Do you have any weapons?"

Dom's eyes widened. The last thing he wanted was to be separated from the only thing that gave him comfort. But...

"Yes," he found himself saying. "I've got a handgun in my backpack."

"Sir, you'll need to set your pack down. We're going to check it and return it to you momentarily. Do you understand?"

"Yes."

Another soldier took his pack. Dom watched as they rifled through it before the doctor jerked his chin forward and shone a light in his eyes.

"Have you come in contact with the parasite in any form?"

Did the man he killed count? The worms and crazy men chasing them down the alley? Seeing his friend be consumed by them? "No."

"Are you traveling with anyone who has come in contact with the parasite?"

"No."

The man pulled Dom's shirt up and prodded at his stomach. His gloved hands felt rough and calculated. He stepped back and nodded to the soldiers. "Clean. Next."

Dom still saw spots of light and dark from the flashlight in his eyes as he donned his pack again, feeling disoriented. It felt much lighter and he wondered if they'd taken anything else beside the gun. Before he left, the doctor put a green tag around his neck.

The soldier led him past at least a dozen more curtained areas before the fence opened up. He was at the end of the T, the middle school in front of him blazing with lights and buzzing with activity as people were ushered in, soldiers patrolling the area.

Dom slowed his pace, scanning the area behind him for Chelsea.

Not again. No, no, no...

Not one of the people trickling from Gate 1 was Chelsea. He'd lost her. Again.

He deviated from the crowd he'd been walking with to the school, looping around in hopes of staying near the gate longer in case she came out. Was it possible she got out before him? Did she tell them something that aroused suspicion?

"Excuse me, Sir, have you been checked?"

Dom spun around, coming face to face with a duo of soldiers.

"Yeah. Uh, see?" He fished his tag out, which was covered by the straps of his pack. "I'm looking for my girlfriend. She was right behind me, and—"

"You need to pass Gate 2 and go into the school."

"I know, but—"

"Sir, I'm not fuckin' askin'. If you don't get a move on, I'm authorized to remove you from the premises."

Dom's jaw hung open. He took another look behind him, not moving.

The other soldier stepped forward. A kid his age, maybe even younger. "Buddy, people get separated at Gate 1, but I can almost guarantee you you'll find her when you get in there." His eyes became distant. "If you don't continue to Gate 2, we have to release you back into the city."

Release him into the city? Don't follow orders and you get tossed to the infected?

"Ok. Fine." He started walking to the school.

"And hey, buddy? Make sure you have your tag showing." The soldier grimaced. "You don't want us thinking you're one of them."

***

Dom was assigned to the theater room to 'wait pending evac.' He was lumped into a group of about thirty people being led through the middle school by an escort of five soldiers. The school was packed. Either they were simply overloaded, or they hadn't been evacuating people yet.

Whatever the case, people were afraid. Dom heard it in the whispered conversations around him. Saw it in the way people eyed the exits. The same thing was on everyone's mind; if only a couple infected got in, it would all be over. They'd be making it easy for them.

When they arrived at the theater room it was half full. All of the seats had been taken, and many people were on stage laying on the floor or sitting. Dom branched off from the main group towards a side wall.

"Please remain calm while we sort out the evacuation procedures. The buses will be arriving shortly." The soldier's voice was flat. "Do not leave this room unless a soldier has okay'd it and is escorting you."

With that he left. The double doors slammed shut. Through the tiny windows Dom saw some of the soldiers remain, keeping guard outside. It made him feel safer. At least they weren't being packed like sardines and left alone.

He shrugged off his pack and sat down, pressing his back against the wall. He felt the weight of Chelsea's absence overtake him. He dropped his head into his hands and inhaled deeply. At least they were in a safe place. They might be separated, but this was different than earlier. There were military guys protecting them. They were moments away from being bussed to a safe zone.

"Mind if I sit down?"

A man stood beside him clutching a suitcase. He wore rumpled, dirty clothes that looked like he hadn't changed them in days. His glasses were tinted a dark shade of brown. A business-like haircut was mussed. His eyes darted from Dom to everyone else in the room and back again. Something about him was familiar, but Dom couldn't place him.

"I guess." Dom scooted aside, dragging his pack between his legs. "Be my guest."

"My name is Adam Baker," he said, holding out his hand.

Dom stared at the offer but didn't take it. Was this guy insane? There was a parasite running rampant that infected people easier than...well, anything Dom had ever heard of.

"I'm Dom," he said. "Sorry, don't really feel great about touching other people. What with everything going on and all."

Adam grinned. "Smart."

"What's with the glasses?"

"Ah, yes. Transition lenses." He adjusted his glasses, pushing them up his nose. "Eventually they simply don't transition back."

"Right."

They sat in silence for a beat before Dom asked, "How long have you been here?"

"Here?" Adam drummed a beat on the top of his suitcase. "A while. Not sure really."

Out of all the refugees, why did Dom have to sit next to the weirdo? But he was here and he was going to make the best of it. "I just got here. I arrived with my girlfriend but we got separated at Gate 1."

"Gate 1?"

"Yeah, where they check you for the parasite."

"Oh, right. Of course. Did you try calling her?"

Call her? Dom mentally slapped himself. He unzipped his backpack and rifled around for his phone. He checked each compartment. It was gone.

"I guess they took it. I had a gun, too. But they took that. Not sure what else they took."

Adam's gaze turned towards the double doors. He didn't have anything to add. Dom pulled a protein bar from his backpack and unwrapped it.

"Anyway, my best hope is that we get on the same bus when they evac us. Or we'll at least meet up once we get to wherever they're taking us."

"There aren't any buses coming."

He stopped chewing. The food felt like a lump of dirt in his mouth. He forced himself to swallow it and turned to face Adam. "What?"

"I've been here since the military took over. Not a single bus has come. Either they're really held up somewhere, or they just aren't coming."

"You're crazy."

Adam pointed above them to the windows. "The entire fleet of yellow school buses are in the lot behind us. They could use those. They haven't."

Dom stood up and peeled one of the blinds down. Sure enough, across the tennis and basketball courts was the school bus lot. A handful of soldiers were patrolling the perimeter of the school. Dom's mind had wanted to justify it by saying they didn't know, but they sure as hell did.

"But they're bombing the city! They can't keep us locked in here, this is in the blast radius."

"The city is trying to separate healthy people from those infected with the parasite. I believe it is a preventative measure, to stop the parasite from spreading. Remove healthy individuals, and perhaps they'll be able to whittle through the infected easier."

"That makes sense, but you're ignoring the huge 'they're going to bomb Seattle' thing.'"

Adam leaned in. He reeked of body odor and stale food. "Do you see that man sitting in the middle of the stage?"

Dom looked. A burly looking guy sat there with whom Dom assumed were his wife and two kids. They wore camouflage and looked tough in a way that made Dom want to avoid them. "What about them?"

"I spoke to him when he first arrived hours ago. He claimed he had enough food, medical supplies, and firepower to get him through anything. I bet he did. One of those doomsday people. He would've stuck it out through everything, but bombs? He said the military blocked off all exits in the blast radius except the ones they're at. They're pooling everyone in these 'evacuation points' as a way of organizing them. He didn't have an option but to come here."

Miles away, Dom's supplies stood neat and stacked in his apartment. The very same apartment he should never have left if what this Adam guy said was true.

"If you're saying the bombing is a huge lie, you're insane. Everything you just told me is a big guess anyway. They're blocking off exits to the city to make things more orderly."

"Or to ensure the flow of people to their designated checkpoints."

"There isn't anything suspicious about it." Dom reassessed Adam. If anything was suspicious, it was him. "Even if they did lie, they're still saving people's lives by trying to stop infection."

Adam leaned against the wall. He tapped his suitcase in rapid succession. "You could look at it that way. But they did it to strike fear and urgency into people. Look at Mr. Survival over there. He wouldn't have left his house if he didn't have to. I'm sure thousands of people would think the same way and, eventually, they'd get killed. The parasite spreads. If everyone thinks they're going to die, they'll all come this way."

The front doors opened and a new group of people were let in. About the same number as in Dom's group. The theater room was filling up quickly. Not many more could fit comfortably without it getting overcrowded. He watched for Chelsea, but as the doors shut and she wasn't in the group, Dom felt his hope deflate. He sighed and stared at the ground.

"Two obvious flaws with that plan," Dom said. "The infected are bound to come to all the checkpoints, too.

When the healthy people come here they'll start getting picked off by the infected. And the infected will come here, too."

"Exactly." Adam had a fervor in his voice at the prospect of death that disturbed Dom.

"And second," Dom continued, "there were only eleven 'evacuation points.' They can't fit the population of the Seattle area in them. What are they going to do? Start turning people away?"

Adam shrugged. "Exactly. Whatever they think they're doing, it is an act of desperation. They *won't* be able to accommodate the numbers. They certainly *don't* have enough manpower to successfully filter each infected individual. Eventually the parasite will take over Seattle, just like every city it's come through so far, and these 'evac points' will be fuel for the fire. Plus, do you know how unlikely it is the military would get authorization to bomb an *entire* city? Even if they actually wanted to, it would take weeks—months!—to get clearance for such a dramatic measure."

As crazy as the guy seemed, something about it all struck true to Dom. The vague statements by the soldiers about when buses were coming, plus the reality of the military bombing the city? He felt embarrassed he didn't question it. But why would he have questioned it? A million thoughts swirled in his mind as waves of emotion overtook him.

He regretted coming here. He was miserable not knowing if Chelsea was safe. He was becoming increasingly uncomfortable with how little he felt in the grand scheme of things.

"How the fuck do you know all this?" Getting angry felt good, even if it was at a total stranger. It felt like a Brian move, and he could see why he always did it. "It

161

makes sense, sure, but it could be a total conspiracy theory."

"I work for the CDC. I know procedure and protocol and none of this checks out."

TV! That's where Dom recognized him from. He made one of the early announcements from the CDC about the infection, which was then thought of as some crazy virus. Only then he looked much more put together. And hadn't he been reporting from...what, Georgia?

"What are you doing here? Shouldn't you be figuring out a cure or something?"

Chewing on his lip, Adam ran his fingers along his suitcase. "I was working on a few things when the campus I was on was overrun with infected. I barely escaped with my life."

The doors opened. Dom looked over, scanning the crowd...

"Chelsea!"

He was on his feet in an instant, pushing through the disgruntled crowd. The look of relief on her face made his heart lift. He took her in his arms for only a moment when the soldiers told them to clear the doorway.

"What took you so long?" Dom asked, gripping her hand in his as he led her to his spot. "Are you okay?"

"I went behind a curtain. They started asking me questions and when they asked if I'd been in contact with the parasite I said yes." She lowered her voice for the last bit, looking around at the crowd. "But that was the *wrong* answer. They asked me where and when, who it was, if I touched them, and a billion other questions I didn't know the answers to."

Dom sat her down, placing himself between Adam and her. He saw the green tag hanging on Chelsea's neck. "But they cleared you?"

"Sure, eventually. I think it was only because someone was throwing a fit about them taking her tablet away behind the curtain next to me. Then I heard soldiers mention a lot of them outside of the evacuation zone." She hugged her arms around her knees. "God, Dom. I think there might be a ton of infected surrounding this area."

To his side, Adam snorted then laughed. "Told you."

Chelsea leaned forward, eyeing him. "Hi?"

"Uh, this is Adam. Just met him."

Dom breathed slowly as he debated whether or not he should tell Chelsea what he now suspected; what crazy Adam had been saying.

Then it all came out. Faster than the conversation with Adam since he subtracted all the conjecture. It was a consolidated version but as Chelsea listened to it, it became evident she was ready to accept it.

"When I walked past the gym down the hall, there was a fight going on. Some guys were arguing, but it looked like it was getting physical. The soldiers were just starting to intervene as I went by." Chelsea squeezed her eyes shut. "I think we made the wrong choice coming here. I really do, Dom. I think we need to leave."

Before Dom could agree with her, the first series of gunshots rang, sending the entire crowd into a panic.

36 Sadie

Getting past the evacuation zone was much easier than Sadie anticipated. Their gates were overwhelmed, and there were actually side streets they hadn't blocked off. She skirted around the massive crowd pressing against each other and was quickly alone, her footsteps sounding loud on the concrete as she walked.

"Whadda you got there, mommy?"

Sadie's blood ran cold. Her hair stood on end as she froze. Her brain told her to run, but her body wouldn't listen.

"She asked what you got there," another female voice said.

In front of her, three women slipped from behind a delivery truck. The streetlight cast a sickly yellow glow across their faces. Up until that point, Sadie hadn't seen live infected people. She'd heard them. Seen glimpses of them from afar, but never this close.

Their eyes were demonic, the grins on their faces unbearable. Blood splattered their clothing and they each carried knives. One raised her head and sniffed.

She wanted to reach for the gun in the side pocket of her backpack, but she couldn't support Jon with one arm. She stood stone still, gaping at the infected.

"That boy is one of us," she said.

"She's got him tied up, that fucking bitch."

"Child abuse!" one screeched, rushing forward.

Sadie found her feet and spun around, running straight for the evacuation zone. There were people there with guns. She couldn't do this on her own. In that moment a primal voice in her head took over. Fear propelled her through a narrow alley that cut through to the evac zone. The burst of adrenaline gave her new strength; she grasped Jon in one hand and reached back, yanking the revolver free from the backpack.

The glow of the huge lamps was just in view when sharp pain brought her to her knees as the first stab entered her back. One of the infected women grabbed her hair, yanking it up as another tore Jon from her arms. The third came in front of her, crouching down to make eye contact.

They didn't realize she had a gun. Sadie brought it up, squeezing the trigger as many times as she could. The back of the woman's head burst as the bullet entered through her eye, splattering the concrete behind them.

But the pain from the stab wound was too much. Sadie collapsed, putting up as much of a fight as she could when they pried the gun from her hand. Neither seemed upset by the loss of their companion.

"You're a bad mommy," one shouted, spit flying into Sadie's face. "You're. A. Bad. Mommy." With each word her knife entered Sadie's stomach, blood pumping from the wounds.

The woman holding her hair let go, sending Sadie to the ground. All she could think about was Jon, her little boy, and how…how maybe she was a bad mother. It was her fault, all of it. His getting sick. Her taking him from home. And Brett. Everything was her fault, everything…she was so close…

"Are you my mommies?"

Sadie inhaled a wet breath. She turned her head, face scratching the concrete as she strained to see her boy. Her vision was darkening, coldness creeping up her limbs.

The women had cut his restraints. He stood near her, looking up at the trio of infected. They stroked his hair, his little arms.

"Yes," one said. "We're good mommies."

The one that stabbed her turned, looking down the alley. The right side of her body jittered violently. "Claudine, he can get in. We can go around the back; no one will see us. We'll slip him through the bathroom windows and he can get all those healthy fuckers in the school."

"Good idea. Hey kiddo, mommies want to give you a boost into that school there. What do you say?"

"Ok," his sweet voice replied. He looked at Sadie, with no recognition in his eyes.

Sadie welcomed death.

37 Adam

It was silly, Adam thought, how gullible people were. Transition lenses. Really? And didn't the kid notice he didn't have a green tag? He knew he was like that at one point, too. It made him like this Dom guy more. He seemed honorable, so concerned with saving his girlfriend, but was realistic enough to accept Adam's logic about the bombing (which was all true, no lies there). The gullible part was what made him a great candidate to replace Marla. In a way, his girlfriend would replace Marla, too. Though Dom obviously didn't know anything about science, his attitude would go far.

Marla.

She had been fun in many ways. After a day on the road he couldn't resist it any longer. He pulled over and had her on the side of the road. The front of her body was almost shredded from being rubbed against the concrete highway, but it was amazing for him. It would be for her soon, too. Obviously the parasite would be transmitted via his semen, then Marla would be like him.

But she hadn't. While they were on the freeway she managed to open the car door. She looked back at him with contempt so pure it almost caused a flicker of guilt within Adam.

"I'll never be like you. *Ever.*"

Even though he slammed on the brakes the moment it happened, she'd flung herself out. Still attached to the door, her body was dragged on the pavement at 75 mph long enough to break her legs and cause massive damage to her body.

Adam took off her cuffs, her dying body limp and heavy, and left her on the highway. Much to his irritation, beneath the blood and gore, her face seemed serene. Rather than letting the parasite take over her body, she chose suicide.

But that was the end of Marla, her reasons ultimately meaning nothing to Adam. If she didn't want to achieve perfection as he had, so what? Perhaps not everyone was meant to.

When he arrived in Seattle a day later, he discovered his old apartment building and its adjacent properties had been leveled to make way for a middle school. At that point Adam almost suffered from a mental collapse. His brain lapsed in and out of being able to think logically. Not having his old apartment back seemed like the most horrific thing in the world.

Adam went inside and trashed a few classrooms to release his rage before he realized it wasn't too big of a deal. He was back in Seattle, his home, and still had all his notes and samples. He just needed to find a good place to settle in and begin researching. If Seattle ended up anything like the infected states he drove through, he merely had to wait things out. They seemed like ghost towns, but within the woodwork survivors and infected alike were teeming. Once it quieted, he'd break into one of the college chemistry departments and begin his work.

But after he resolved to get himself together, the military showed up and started taking over the middle school. Adam had no choice but to hide, fearful of what they'd do when they found him. He hid underneath the theater room stage, gleaning information from soldiers and refugees as they started piling in. Once there were enough of them, Adam exited his hiding place to figure out how to escape.

It didn't take long for him to figure out he couldn't leave without a big diversion. Lucky for him, he didn't have to make one. As soon as the infected came through the door, the room's inhabitants swarmed towards any exit they could think of. Chairs were thrown at windows, many rushed the double doors and tried pressing through the infected trying to come in.

Adam knew of an emergency exit behind the stage. Not many refugees went back there, and sure enough, as he led Dom and his girlfriend back, there were only a few people darting through it. More would come once they caught on.

He led them through, utilizing his basic knowledge of the layout from when he first arrived, and exited out the side of the middle school. People ran in all directions, going anywhere as long as it was away from the school.

"Where are we going?" Dom asked, raising his voice above the chaos behind them.

Adam looked up and down the street, spotting his car where he'd left it. "Down there, my car. Come on!"

They followed him blindly, just as Adam had hoped, and he ushered them into the backseat. It was dark, and hopefully they wouldn't note the smears of blood and handcuffs on the passenger side. If they did, he could easily explain it away.

Or use his gun. The gun fixed a lot of things.

As Adam pulled off the curb and began driving away from the school, he noted Dom in the back seat with his smart phone out. The girl retrieved hers as well.

"Keep going south. The roads don't look too bad according to these traffic cams. If we keep going towards the forest, I think we can..."

The girlfriend lost it. "Dom, we talked about this! We'll die if we go traipsing into the woods hoping to survive this."

169

"I have a friend who lives in…" Adam's voice caught on the lie as he tried to think of a woodsy town south from Seattle. It had been too long since he was in the area. "Black Diamond. It is southeast from here, but I think it's a good place to try and hide if we can make it there."

Dom and Chelsea looked at each other, then Dom agreed to Adam's plan. Were they skeptical? Adam thought he was acting the part well of a nervous survivor.

The next two hours passed in silence as the couple's adrenaline seemed to fade. Adam did know where Black Diamond was; he often hiked alone in the area when he was a teenager. There were many big summer houses in the area. They need only break into one and stay in it until the time was right to come back to Seattle.

Kill them. Eat their skin. Feel their blood.

Adam tried to suppress the violent thoughts, but each time he looked back and saw them, he wanted to do something to hurt them.

I need them, he thought. *I need people to see this thing through.*

Nothing to see. Rape her, make her yours. Make him watch.

Kill her while he watches

Cut off her

Blood on your skin

blood

Adam didn't realize how his body had been twitching, or how his glasses slipped down his nose too far, showing his bloody eyes, or how he'd been saying all the things he wanted to do to them out loud.

He didn't realize it until he felt the muzzle of a gun pressed against his neck and a voice say, "Pull over."

38 Dom

He doesn't have a green tag

The text Chelsea typed out and handed to him made his body tense. The guy, Adam, *didn't* have a tag. Why hadn't Dom noticed that sooner? He was also weird, and now that they were alone with him he seemed even stranger. As Chelsea and Dom sat in the back seat, he made an effort to watch how the man acted.

It didn't take long to realize, now that the heat of the moment had worn off, that he was infected. For the first hour he just drove, calmly navigating the roads and taking them southeast just as he said he would. Then things got weird. He started whispering to himself, his right hand jerking off the steering wheel and back on.

Chelsea typed on her phone again and tilted the screen toward Dom.

There are handcuffs on the door. Blood in the front seat

What had Dom done? How could he have gotten them into such a terrible situation again? He'd just gotten Chelsea back and now he put her life in danger. Was it the confusion of being pushed into the theater room that made him ignore the obvious?

The inclination to blame the military popped into his mind; they should've checked the refugees harder. The very thing they wanted to prevent happened.

When Adam started talking about rape and blood, Dom knew he had to do something. They took turns on her phone, discreetly typing to one another.

Did they take your gun?

No

Get it out. Slowly

Chelsea did. Dom held his breath, waiting for Adam to notice they were doing something in the back seat, but Adam seemed to be unaware of their presence even though he spoke of wearing Dom's skin and doings things to Chelsea that made him want to vomit.

She passed the gun to him. He raised it to Adam's head, hoping the man had enough sense to save his life to pull over instead of wrecking them.

"Pull over."

A heaviness swept over the car. Dom made eye contact in the mirror and repeated the command, but Adam didn't move. All he heard was the car and everyone's breath.

"You don't understand. I have work to do."

"What—shut up. Just shut up and pull over."

"Please, Dom. I know this looks strange, but—"

"Don't say my name! I swear I will pull this trigger and splatter your brains on the windshield."

He grinned. "Would you? Would you risk the blood and brain getting on you and your pretty fucking little whore? It would get inside of you because it's inside of *me*. And you'd die because the car would flip-flippity-flip right off the road when I lose control."

Adam rattled off another string of words, but Dom couldn't make out what he was saying.

"Chelsea, pull your hood on. Get something out of your bag and cover your face."

"What?"

Dom's hand shook as he pressed the gun into Adam's head. "I said cover up. I'm going to shoot him. I don't want any blood to get on us."

The car began slowing down. Adam appeared to be unhappy with Dom's decision. It made Dom feel hopeful, since it was a bluff. He wouldn't shoot Adam, because he was right. They were going over 70 mph. Even if both of them were covered head to toe in a hazmat suit, they'd likely die when Adam lost control.

"I want you to listen to me, please. Listen, and when I'm done I'll stop the car and let you out. If you still want to."

Dom glanced at Chelsea. She'd tightened her hood and wore a scarf around her nose and mouth. Her eyes glittered with tears and fear. She gave him one curt nod.

"Fine. Start talking."

"I know it's hard for you to understand what it's like— having the parasite inside of you. But it isn't as bad as you think. It's helping me think clearer, clearer than I have in *years*. I think it's a potentially glorious next step in the evolution of humans."

Adam spoke with energetic sincerity. His pinky fingers tapped the steering wheel in rapid succession. He licked his lip, a dribble of bile seeping from it down his chin.

"I have a background in biochemistry, you see, and I'm going to find a few likeminded individuals to help tweak some of *Anisakis Nova*'s genetics...the clarity...can't lose the fucking clarity..."

He trailed off into another string of babbles. Some of it sounded like genuine scientific terms, but some weren't words at all.

Then they all honed in on the infected bumbling down the highway straight towards them, its stomach pointed forward and head lolled back.

Adam slammed on the brakes, but it was too late. The car hit the woman at almost top speed, sending her against the windshield and over the car. Fireworks of blood, entrails, and worms burst across the windshield. He jerked the steering wheel to the right. The car spun out of control, spinning wildly down the road.

Chelsea was screaming. Dom was too, holding onto the headrest of the passenger seat as the world blurred around them. Adam's head hung downward, his body moving in time with the motion of the car.

The momentum of the spin petered out. Dom heard his own labored breathing and the ticking of the engine. He smelled burnt rubber. Something warm was seeping into his eye. He blinked away blood from a gash on his right temple.

"Chels...Chelsea?" She was leaning against the door; the only thing keeping her up was her seatbelt. Dom gently took her chin and tilted her head towards him. She was breathing. Her eyes fluttered open, gazing first at Dom then to the front of the car.

Adam hadn't been wearing a seatbelt. His body had been thrown to the passenger side of the car. He wasn't moving, but Dom saw his torso rising and falling with his breath.

"We need to go. Now." Dom clicked his own buckle free, glad the habit to strap in stuck with him even in the chaotic moment when they'd first entered the car. "Can you walk? Are you okay?"

Chelsea nodded, but winced and brought her hand to her neck. She slowly straightened her body and opened the door.

That was all the confirmation he needed. Dom averted his attention to finding the gun, which had flown out of his hands during the wreck. It wasn't anywhere in the back seat. He leaned forward and looked around the front.

There, as far away as it could be, the gun was wedged in the left side of the dashboard. Adam groaned, his body twitching. Dom would have to lean over him to get it.

"Come on, let's go!" Chelsea was completely out of the car, looking in at him expectantly. Then in an instant she was gone. Dom watched in horror as an infected barreled into her, knocking her into the ground.

Any hesitation of getting the gun vanished. He dove forward, over Adam's body, kicking the backseat for momentum. His hand brushed against the gun. He stretched farther. The metal was still warm from his grip only moments before.

Dom scrambled out of the car. Chelsea was doing her best to hold the man at bay, but he flailed at her wildly. Dom kicked his side, knocking him off her and rolling onto the ground.

Pop.

The bullet went into his neck. Blood spurted everywhere. Chelsea turned onto her side just as a jet of it hit her.

Dom took aim again and squeezed. This time the bullet went straight through the infected man's head, brains painting the road behind him as his body collapsed.

"Fuck! Fuck, it's on me!"

Chelsea tore off her backpack and jacket, wiping away at the stray flecks of blood on her skin. As Dom stepped forward to help her, he heard something rustle behind him.

The passenger door was ajar. Adam was gone, running opposite them into the forest on the other side of the road. He raised his gun and took aim, firing a round off before the gun went dry, the bullet not even grazing Adam.

If he wants to run away, let him.

Dom turned and helped Chelsea clean the blood off as best as he could. They needed to find somewhere safe to rest, to get their sanitary wipes out of the packs, to gather themselves, to make a plan...

Dom didn't realize his hands were shaking until Chelsea took them into hers. "We're going to be okay."

Those little words, simple and promising, calmed him. And in that moment, he believed her.

39 Barry

Barry Weinstein had no qualm in admitting he didn't come back to work because he was afraid. He was surprised anybody *did* come to work. It seemed pretty obvious that it was the End of Days, the Apocalypse, Judgment Day. No one should have to do anything when the shit hits the fan, he told himself. He felt sorry for the schmucks who were still dragging themselves in at 8am for the daily grind.

Not Barry. He was a smart guy. He'd won patents and awards, was the favorite among all the upper bureaucrats at work. As soon as he realized holing up in his house increased his chances of surviving, the thought of going back to work was a joke. Barry had it all.

Well, he had everything but courage. He admitted his colleagues risking their safety was courageous; a little part of him wished he could be like that, too.

Since the day he left work he spent his time buying as much food and supplies as he could fit in his car, hauling it back to his modest suburban home, and hiding it throughout the house. He boarded up the windows—he was the first to do it in the neighborhood, starting a trend—and once he felt it was too dangerous to leave his home, he stayed inside.

Inside the dark, lonely, boarded up house.

He thought it would be kind of fun, like some morbid staycation. But he couldn't help checking his work email, where he saw slews of messages going back and forth between his fellow scientists. The live hosts coming in, the emergency break, and then…

Dr. Ainsworth's voicemail.

In the middle of blending his third pitcher of frozen margaritas that day, he didn't hear his cellphone ring. No one had called him in days, and had he heard it, he would've answered. He would've told Marla to be strong, that he would call the police. He would've made all the false promises he needed to if it made her feel safe.

But he didn't. Instead, he settled into his favorite chair with his margarita, not even realizing he had a message until after he watched *The Matrix* for the second time and absentmindedly checked his phone.

I found a cure...

His head swam.

Baker has me hostage, he's infected...

He leaned over his chair and threw his margaritas up right back into the blender.

It took him ten minutes of breathing deeply, staring at his own feet before he picked up the phone and called every form of authority he possibly could, the words, "There's a cure," waiting to escape his lips.

40 Adam

Adam was furious. The rage was almost blinding in its intensity. He cursed at every branch that hit his face during his escape into the forest. His shoes and pants were caked with mud by the time he finally stopped to take a deep breath.

That fucking imbecile, that whore!

He had high hopes for them both. How dare they betray him? How dare they try and stop him from doing what the world needed? What was right? They had almost killed him. He heard the bullet thud as it hit a tree beside him. They could've ended him.

It was obvious he had to pick his allies more carefully. First Marla, then the couple. Adam was inclined to think it was because they weren't infected yet. If they were, he knew they'd see things his way. It was impossible to deny the urges and strength the parasite created once it coursed inside your body.

He made a note to infect all future potential friends, or only befriend them to begin with. Yet the problem was each infected had a variety of dispositions. Some were exploders, others too insane to reason with. It might be a challenge to find the right mix. A challenge, but not impossible.

Adam looked around him. Nothing but pine trees and ferns as far as he could see. He finally realized he had no idea where he was, let alone what direction he'd been traveling in. The sun was almost gone, sending the forest into an eerie, quiet state of twilight.

What a disaster. Fucking disaster. Dis-fucking-aster...

"Get it together!" the power in his voice sent a chill through his body. He began walking, ignoring fatigue and hunger. He would get to where he needed to go. There was no other option.

The future rested on him. All the millions of infected roaming the country, uncoordinated and fighting the battle for supremacy; they needed a leader. They needed someone on their side who could make them stronger. Someone who could direct their efforts.

Each of them was a beat in the pulse of a new dominant species. Soon, the entire world would be united by the parasite.

Soon, they would be One.

Eloise J. Knapp

41 Dom

Since the infection started, Dom had been waiting. He was waiting to be saved. For it to all go way. To escape. To give up. To die.

But now that he stood a chance of making it—now that he was away from the chaos of the world he knew collapsing into nothing—he was numb.

This was only the beginning. There wasn't a doubt in his mind that the parasite was crossing the seas, if it hadn't already, and would soon dominate the entire world. How humanity existed would change forever. Whatever mattered before, whatever he worried about or looked forward to...

Dom glanced at Chelsea, passed out from exhaustion. The meager campfire they managed to start cast shadows and light across her sleeping body. Her face, smeared with dirt and sweat, was serene. At peace.

A bit of warmth flickered within him.

Whatever mattered before *still* did. He still loved her, more than ever after what they'd been through. Whatever *this* was, they could do it. They escaped their apartment, the evacuation zone, and Adam. After a day hiking through the forest, sticking close to roads, they'd managed to survive without too many hardships.

He wasn't sure where they'd end up, but they were strong.

They would survive.

Epilogue

It seemed there was no hope. Two months after the initial outbreak, *Anisakis Nova's* reach extended into every continent. For every healthy, living person fighting, there were ten infected there trying to kill them. Despite the effort from the military and government, without a cure or vaccination, it was a matter of time before any chance of survival went to zero.

The world held its breath as more died or became infected, as life came to a grinding halt.

When the first rounds of MAC—*Marla Ainsworth's Cure,* named after the woman who laid the groundwork down for it—were administered successfully in Georgia, no one knew. The power grid was down, servers crashed or destroyed, and the ability to communicate across states was nearly impossible.

But a spark ignited the world's sense of hope. The super antihelminthic was produced en masse around the world. Helicopters dropped it off by the crateful in major cities. The military rallied, their second wind something that would be forever marked in history books, defending hospitals and MAC dispensing locations with a kind of zeal that saved the country. Slowly the number of infected decreased until only a handful of areas remained hazardous.

Yet questions remained unanswered. The CDC released MAC without a full understanding of its potential ramifications. They were authorized to administer MAC only because the need for it was dire. Since the drug worked it would be sending humanity to certain death if they didn't. As soon as the country stabilized, the CDC went into overdrive, researching genetics of *Anisakis Nova* and MAC's effect on it.

The consequences of the near-doomsday were everywhere. Fires had raged out of control, wiping out cities and neighborhoods. Millions of people were still unaccounted for, presumed dead or infected. The country people once knew was gone, operating on a skeleton crew of only the most basic workforces to provide electricity, water, and food.

But *Anisakis Nova's* devastation was far from over. It was always darkest before dawn.

Acknowledgements

Around 2010 I watched an episode of *River Monsters* about a worm that eats you from the inside out. The idea stuck with me. It wasn't until years later after I had a dream in which people were exploding worms from their stomachs that I knew I wanted to revolve a novel around the concept. Thanks to all my family members who listened to me repeatedly describe the dream and watch me as I did the "and then the parasite explodes from their chest cavity" gesture while explaining the novel.

Thanks to Jamie Northam for the title, my beta readers for bearing through the drafts and their honest feedback, and John MacLeod for his editing.

Huge thank you to all my fans who were willing to let me "kill them" in this book. Sorry to those who I didn't get to; your time will come.

Matt Scholz, thank you for all your "sciency" input!

And of course, to all my fans who take the time to enter these crazy worlds I write; without you, I'm just a crazy person typing words on the computer.

About Eloise J. Knapp

Knapp lives in Washington state and never complains about the rain. She went to Seattle University for graphic design and creative writing. If she isn't crafting tales of the apocalypse, Knapp enjoys hot yoga, frequenting the movie theater, and preparing for the end of the world. Other works include The Undead Situation and The Undead Haze published by Permuted Press.

Get Connected

Reviews mean a lot to authors. They help us grow, motivate us, and, of course, helps sell more books! This is especially true in the case of self-published work. Please take a moment to leave a review. I read each one of them and appreciate any feedback, praise, or criticism you may have to offer.

Connect
www.eloisejknapp.com
www.facebook.com/eloisejknapp
@EloiseJKnapp

More by Eloise J. Knapp

The Undead Situation (Permuted Press)

The Undead Haze (Permuted Press)

Available in ebook, paperback, and audiobook.

A Sample From
THE UNDEAD SITUATION

By Eloise J. Knapp

The dead are rising. People are dying.
Civilization is collapsing.

When the end finally occurred, everything about it was
cinematic. The dead came back and ate people, civilization
collapsed, and no one could do a thing.

But Cyrus V. Sinclair couldn't care less; he's a sociopath.

Amidst the chaos, Cyrus sits back and contemplates the
gore stained streets and screams of his fellow man with
little more emotion than one of the walking corpses. With
his cache of guns and MREs, he rather likes the idea of
hunkering down in his Seattle apartment
while the world ends outside.

All is well and good for Cyrus… until he meets up with
Gabe, a belligerent annoyance, and the other inconvenient
survivors who cramp his style and force him to re-evaluate
his outlook on life. It's Armageddon, and things will
definitely get messy.

Well, it happened.

When it did happen, everything about it was cinematic. I'm sure people banded together and tried to save themselves from their untimely dooms. They found solace in a mall, a house, or bunker, just like in the movies. Desperation and pessimism just prevented them from seeing the film-like qualities of their actions.

I was sitting in my apartment, alone, when it happened. Downstairs I could hear the banging of pots and pans as people fixed dinner. Their kids were whining, but that wasn't anything unusual.

Outside the sky was plagued with deep grey clouds, rain pouring. I left the window open so I could hear the softness of it.

A train whistled across town. A cop car, sirens blaring, sped past the front of my apartment building. I listened to its sound fade away, again leaving me with the noises of my home and of rain.

It happened all at once, taking the entire world by storm. It happened so quickly, people didn't believe it was true. Denial just made the undead count rise alarmingly fast. People who accepted it were considered crazy by those who didn't. In the end, I bet everyone wished they'd seen a few more Romero movies, maybe been a little less close minded.

If I were to try and tell you exactly how the whole zombie thing spread, I'd probably have to make up some stuff. No one knew if it was a disease or infection, or why it also made you turn when you died from non-Z related injuries. Oh, experts—especially religious experts—had a jolly good time with their theories, but no one truly knew what was going on. So, as I sat alone in my apartment, the chaos-inducing news of the zombies finally spread to Seattle, Washington.

People died then they came back. They ate other people. It's a cliché way of putting it, but it's the absolute truth.

There was only one person I knew who would accept the news as quickly as me—my long time friend Francis. He called early on with the latest update on the situation outside.

"You're supposed to quarantine anyone who's been bit, did you know that?"

"I hadn't heard."

"Boy, don't you turn on the TV?"

"You know I don't have a TV."

The apocalypse *was* now, and since Frank and I were alike we both accepted that without much thought. I wasn't sure what Frank's plan was, but I got out my box of old Guns & Ammo for entertainment, barricaded my apartment door, and cracked open a can of sweetened condensed milk for the ride. (I've got a sweet tooth. Sue me.)

With my canned goods obscene in calories and a top-story view of Seattle, I watched people die. I watched stuff blow up, stuff break, and the zombies gain numbers for their undead ranks.

My name is Cyrus V. Sinclair, and I didn't care.

Chapter 1

I wasn't going to leave.

I was going to leave.

Only days after the outbreak started, downtown Seattle was in a state of chaos and disrepair. From my window I watched people from all walks of life, all shapes and sizes, and of all colors get eaten by their fellow man. Some people thought zombie movies were graphic, but nothing was as stunning as watching the action in real life.

Really, I suppose everyone's intestines tasted the same. Discrimination wasn't an issue once you were a zombie.

A fully loaded military grade pack waited by the front door. When I packed it, I had intentions to leave. That was when rumors of the dead rising started. Now the dead *had* risen and I was still sitting in my apartment, hesitant to make a decision. Just one decision. But instead of deciding, I was thinking about the world outside.

I decided we were all doomed for sure, and maybe that's why I hadn't stepped outside of my apartment in almost two weeks. Before, there was a chance of survival; the military was still trying to get control of things, the electricity was always on, and most people were still acting like…like people. But once the lights started flickering and occasionally went out, casting the whole city into complete suppressive darkness, I knew it would be just me, myself, and I 'til the end of days. My ferret, Pickle, was my only companion who would accompany me for the apocalypse. For days we shared comfortable silence, eating gummy bears and ferret food, watching the mass destruction of mankind unfold before us.

The monotonous days were broken up by phone calls from Frank. My cell vibrated on the kitchen counter. He spoke before I could even say hello.

"How bad is it there?"

I didn't have a TV, internet, or interaction with other people, so my personal opinion was limited. "Not too bad. The power's still on, plumbing works mostly, and apparently I get reception."

Frank huffed. "Well, I'll *tell* you how bad it is. The coast is overrun. No ships coming in or out. A man going east told me he saw freighters ramming into shore. Goes without saying everyone is killing each other, living or dead. Damn government said they're taking appropriate measures."

It was surprising how fast civilization fell apart. One minute we were haughty Americans, the next we were as bad off as every other human being on planet Earth. Despite the government's claims they could save everyone, or they were taking "appropriate measures," people went berserk and the world went straight to Hell.

"Doesn't matter what everyone else is doing. I'm fine here," I said.

"You're still in the apartment? How long are you planning on staying there?"

How was I supposed to know? One minute I was ready to walk out the door, and the next I was ready to hole up in the apartment forever. "I don't plan on staying here. I've been thinking about leaving."

"Well, lucky for you, you don't have to think about it anymore. I'm coming to get you."

I masked a gasp with a choke. Keeping my voice level, I asked, "What are you talking about? I thought you were still in Little Rock?"

Frank, in few words, explained that I couldn't take care of myself worth a damn and he was going to pick me up.

His parents, survivalists like Francis, left him a cabin in the mountains which he'd been working on for the past year. That meant Frank had been in Washington for a year without coming to see me. I felt a little hurt, but didn't mention it.

"I'm not the same teenager who showed up on your doorstep, Frank. I can handle myself."

The static of the phone almost masked it, but I heard him snort in disbelief. "Never said you were. So you're saying no to the cabin?"

I knew I wasn't thinking it through, but pride overtook me. Frank was an honorable man, and he was only looking out for me. But I couldn't stand the idea of someone thinking I couldn't take care of myself. I just couldn't.

"That's right. I've got a plan and I'm sticking to it."

"You've got a plan? You just said yo—"

The cell made a horrific high pitched squeal before going silent. No automated voice explained the phenomenon.

That was the last time I used a phone.

A few days after talking to Frank, I regretted my decision. His intention was noble and I shot him down. Our conversation was probably our last, and I acted like a complete ass. My pack was still resting by the door, and I visualized it mocking me for saying no. Then the bag reminded me of how I met Francis. I was sobered by the thought.

In 1993, when I was 16, my grandparents and I had just moved to Little Rock, Arkansas. At that point I was 'just too far gone.' The epitome of a no-good punk. Unwanted, I packed my few belongings and ran away. I wasn't smart and didn't know the area, so I unintentionally hiked up into the Ozarks.

I found myself on the property of Francis Jackson Bordeaux with a shotgun pointed at me. Frank was a Vietnam veteran with a mean case of Post Traumatic Stress Disorder.

Long story short, I lived with him for about a year until I moved onto another chapter of my life. I learned a lot from Francis J. Bordeaux, almost everything that mattered.

I thought about Frank's personality, how when I lived with him and I said no, he took no as yes every time. A part of me believed, despite my harsh refusal, he was still coming to get me.

He was, I decided. There was no way he'd changed enough *not* to come get me. That was when my plan was set; I would turtle up in my apartment until Frank came. Until then, it was the same old routine. Watch outside, maintain inside.

Frank opened my eyes to how bad things were in the city. Instead of just looking, I analyzed the situation. The entire city was clearly on its way to complete destruction. Looters took advantage of the turmoil and broke into every shop they could. Even the windows of the children's toy store across the street were shattered, dollies and teddy bears strewn everywhere.

Despite not leaving the apartment (or maybe because of it), my body was still fresh and lithe. I hadn't spent a single day running away from animated corpses or fighting my way through hordes of the living trying to escape to a different fate. At twenty-seven, I was as spry as any teenager, maybe even more so. (Undoubtedly, my laidback personality had something to do with it.)

As I walked through my two-bedroom one-bath residence, I took mental note of its state. The kitchen and dining room were both sparsely furnished. Someone would think an inhabitant was nonexistent. The short hallway and bedrooms were stark, void of any personal expression. The only signs of human existence were empty canned goods on the kitchen counter, an H&K PSG-1 towering among the empty bags of candy in the dining room, and a scatter of Frank Sinatra records resting on the living room floor with the record player.

There were many places I'm sure I could have gone to get some goods. There was a convenience store down the street that offered all the candy I could eat. (One might wonder how it's possible for me to live on sugar. The answer was this: I don't.) My bedroom overflowed with MRE's (Meals Ready to Eat), the flavorful choice of the U.S. military. Although their flavor wasn't as delicious as a roll of Life-Savers, it kept me running.

Call me crazy, but I knew some kind of apocalypse would happen in my lifetime. I wasn't necessarily preparing for the undead, but stocking up on MREs over time seemed like a good idea anyway. Stockpiling gun after gun since I was sixteen? Well, that was just a hobby.

After moseying into the eating area, checking what I did have left food-wise, I went back to the balcony to assess the corpse situation. The spring air was impregnated with the stench of rotting flesh, a scent not unbearably unpleasant, and within that the electric undertone of a lightning storm soon to come. The street had emptied. I guessed the dead had better luck indoors, where people might still be hiding, so they went hunting inside.

A mom and pop grocery store stood across the street from my building, next to the book store. It looked thoroughly looted. Windows were nonexistent and rotting corpses lay on the ground. I figured there had to be some sweets still available in there, though. Who went for things like candy when the mindless dead were seeking them out?

No one, of course, but I got grouchy without a good sugar fix. I was also bored and wanted to leave.

Even though the streets looked abandoned, there was no way the undead weren't waiting in the shadows for lunch to come strolling by. I'd have to be cautious.

A simple backpack would suffice for raiding. It was big enough to hold a lot, but wouldn't get too heavy and weigh me down. After a thorough search of my apartment, I dug up a crowbar to use as a silent melee weapon. I was taking my 9mm, not because I was trigger happy but because it was necessary. Despite my abundance of ammo, using the gun would only draw more attention. A gun shot was a dinner bell; one I didn't want to ring.

Weeks had passed since I had last left the apartment. I wasn't sure I could step out of it without being eaten alive by the pesky undead. But I had to try.

After unlocking the three deadbolts and removing the extra wooden plank across my door, I peeked out. The hallway was scattered with random junk and the walls were smeared with dried blood. Only one or two of the apartments were open. Down the hallway was an elevator next to emergency stairs. The elevator was partially closed, with half a corpse wedged between its doors. The door to the stairs was closed.

When I passed the open doors, I shut them as quietly as possible. I wasn't sure if zombies could open doors, but it wouldn't hurt to close them. One of the rooms revealed a man, an undead bag of skin and bones, who had apparently hanged himself early on. His throat was torn up, but he still tried to groan in relief at the sight of me. He swayed as he tried to come after me, overwhelmed that a meal finally stumbled his way. The rope was Kevlar, a material he'd often expressed fondness for. Between the quality of the rope and his barely existent weight, I wasn't surprised he was still hanging.

His name was Rick Johnson, I remembered, as I stared at his face. Years ago, when I moved into the apartment, he tried desperately to invite me to dinner to meet his daughter. My lack of interest ended in a fight, after which we never spoke to one another again. That suited me just fine.

I shut that door, writing Rick and that story off all together.

Except for a dull thudding noise behind Apartment 8's door, the creaking of Hang-Man's rope, everything was quiet. The silence was ominous, especially when I considered what horrors lay behind the closed doors. My mind ramped up with thoughts of ghouls eating themselves as a last resort, or just standing around in the rooms forever, or at least until someone came and killed them.

My luck held, and I made it down the flights of stairs without incident. The main and only entrance to the apartment wasn't broken in any way, but why would it be? There wasn't really anything to loot in here. Someone would have to be desperate to raid a low-class apartment building like mine.

Before I left the lobby downstairs, I studied the street from my new ground view. Paper and dark blood coated the sidewalks and the street. I could barely make out the asphalt from all the debris. There were body parts everywhere. Half a torso here, an arm there. One lower half still twitched, but since it couldn't do me any harm, I didn't care.

The carnage was interesting to look at—in a modern art kind of way—but I didn't want to spend too much time surveying. This mission was a run in run out kind of deal. No matter how long I waited, or how hard I looked, they'd still be there.

Slowly, I pushed the door open and slipped through, glancing up and down the street. A single zombie stumbled out of a clothing boutique, but hadn't noticed me yet. His arms were gone, with only a few scraggly tendons and nerves left dangling from sockets. A hideous smashing of skin, bone, and muscle made up his face. I doubted he could even see, so I took advantage of his oblivion and made a dash across the street.

My boots slapped against the ground and echoed loudly. It couldn't be prevented, but the noise made me cringe. Running was a zombie's second favorite noise. It meant breakfast, lunch, or dinner. Maybe all three. (A Zs favorite noise was people screaming—that generally meant he got lucky.)

The grocery smelled foul before I even went inside. A thick scent bombarded me, choking me as it hit in waves. It wasn't just the smell of rotting food. A body I had spotted earlier was slimy and covered in maggots. This one had been dead for a considerably long time and was extra gooey. (I never knew organs took on such bizarre colors when rotted.)

With my back pressed against the wall, I turned and peered through the corner of the broken window. I couldn't spot any Zs above the short aisles, but they could be crawling or crouched too low for me to see. The whole place was the poster child of an apocalypse. Only a few items remained on the shelves. Rotting dairy products had turned green after falling from the refrigerators. There was a puddle of curdled green goop just beyond the doorway. I tried to breathe through my mouth and not acknowledge the stench.

Without thinking twice, I jogged into the store, stepping carefully as to avoid the wet patches on the ground. I shrugged my pack off and unzipped it, keen on shoving in as many goodies as possible. The candy section was practically untouched, save for a lone arm rotting near Snickers bars.

Glancing around, I pilfered Life Savers and listened intently for any zombies. A soft squeaking caught my attention as I stuffed Hostess cupcakes and Twinkies in the top of my backpack. As the squeaking grew louder, my pilfering sped up.

A torso pulled its way along the floor. It was a woman, once, but I could only tell because of her chest. Her hair had come off in clumps, leaving behind a ragged, bloody skull. Her face had been scoured off, leaving nothing but tattered gore behind. White, foggy eyes bulged out of her skull. Intestines followed behind her, creating bloody trails on the checkered linoleum floor.

I was quiet. Didn't move a muscle. A slick pool of blood in front of her hindered her progress. Torso Woman ground her teeth in frustration and let out a loud, teetering groan as her arms thrashed about.

Somewhere outside a chorus of replies sounded off, reverberating down the street and into the store. My position had been given away. In a world infested with undead, if there were two entrances, then there was only one exit. The one you came in by would be the one zombies filed in through. For me that meant no exits. My luck with the immobile Torso Woman would run out once other, more capable zombies saw me.

After I zipped and secured the backpack, I approached the woman and killed her with one swift whack from my crowbar. I went to the entrance and took the risk of running straight out.

The armless zombie was steps away from me. I darted past him, scanning the street as I went. Behind him another two followed. To my other side, multiple Zs were staggering out of storefronts, excited by Torso Woman's call.

My apartment was just a walk across the street. If I ran fast enough, I'd be able to shoot right by them without taking time to put them out of their misery. I took that option.

Gnarled hands grabbed at me as I barreled through, wrenching the door open the moment I was close enough. There was no time to lock it since they were right behind me, salivating for my flesh. Adrenaline carried me up the stairs faster than a hunted rabbit.

As I entered the hallway to my apartment, a zombie lunged from the side. My sidestep would've worked if there hadn't been a sour patch of blood and other coagulated liquids resting on the maroon linoleum where my boot struck. Instead, I slipped and fell onto my back, the undead going right with me. His ridged hands clawed at me while he snapped his jaws at my exposed neck. Crowbar long forgotten, I reached into my holster for the 9mm while I held the pus laden beast away. With one burst of strength, I knocked him off and brought up the gun simultaneously, squeezing a bullet into his head. Grabbing the crowbar and holstering the handgun, I scrambled to my feet and rushed down the hallway. All the apartment doors I shut remained shut, except for mine which I had left open.

How could I have done something that dimwitted? I wanted to take my time and check the rooms, but couldn't risk the delay, so I walked straight in, slamming the door shut. After quickly locking the bolts and dropping the extra board into position, I stood still and listened, already questioning my decision to lock up so early. But I'd rather fight one or two Zs trapped inside than the horde coming from outside.

No noises gave away an undead, but that didn't mean one wasn't there. Crowbar on the ready, I glimpsed into my spare room. It was empty, as was the bathroom next to it.

Leaning the other way, I took a step forward, glancing into my bedroom. It, too, was clear.

I went to the end of the hall, which opened up into the living area, and stopped cold. In the corner of the room, near my records, a woman swayed back and forth, facing the wall. Adorned in a tweed business suit with minor rips and stains, she appeared relatively normal. Her hair was still up in a tight bun, revealing mottled gray skin. The only giveaway was a bullet wound through the back of her neck.

She turned around slowly then caught sight of me. Her on switch triggered, she lurched forward, trying to close the distance between us....

27148758R00127

Made in the USA
Charleston, SC
04 March 2014